Prologue

How much more fun could be had exactly? Every variety of man, woman, coupling, tripling (and more), swapping, fantasy and extreme was there on a plate and ready to be taken. The trouble was, Lou already had!

The innocence of discovery was a cliché in her case. The past four years had been anything but pure, unless you wanted to call it 'pure delight', but even that wasn't quite accurate. There had been adventures and misadventures, but equally still, in all of those scenarios, it had been a learning curve of sorts. What was there left to explore and what did she want now? That was becoming a recurring question of late – what actually did Lou desire?

Was it time to cast the swinging aside, to settle down and find 'the one' - if such a man actually existed? Would she ever find someone who could satisfy her fully or had she set the bar too high and prevented herself from ever finding such a person? Given her checkered few years of depravity, would anyone want her anyway?

Before she let 'whatever will be (will be)', there was just a little more steam in her engine to use up first!

CHILLI DIP

Louisa Berry

Copyright © 3P Publishing Ltd
First published in 2020 in the UK
3P Publishing
C E C, London Road
Corby, NN17 5EU

A catalogue number for this book is available from
the British Library

ISBN: 978-1-913-740-01-6

Cover design: Marie-Louise O'Neill

Cover photography by Alan R Horten

For all those readers who are keeping their heads above water, as they continue their silent struggle. You've got this!

Now for some escapism …

Acknowledgments

2019 was a year that taught me many valuable lessons. I learned a lot, but I am also waiting for karma to play her part to those deserving of her. It was difficult to write at times but when I did, I enjoyed escaping into Lou's world and I'm very glad now to be sharing the third installment with you.

So I offer a 'big shout out' to those who stuck with me through thick and thin: Francesca, Carmen, Ethan, Aidan, Tom, Dan, Debs, Lenny, Muna, Mandy, Michelle, Louise, Mark and many others. Thank you for keeping your faith in me as I struggled to maintain mine in others at times! And here we are: stronger, more resilient, humble, grateful, proud and loving life.

Alan, thanks for your superb photography, wise counsel and valued friendship.

Finally a huge thank you to my beautiful family whom I utterly adore and to the new friends I have made following a new passion (yoga). I am truly blessed.

Louisa Berry

Contents:

Chapter 1 - Silky saliva

Rob was based in Luxembourg when he first made contact with Lou. He'd popped onto her online profile and his introduction was way more original than many of the usual, "Hi, how are you?" approaches. It was almost nonchalant and could have been easily ignored if his pictures hadn't struck a chord. He stood at around 6' 3", slim though not muscly, and sported a 'salt and pepper' beard to match his hair. What really won her over was that beautiful, wide smile of his. There was something about him Lou's witchlike inner tendencies instantly liked. He appeared to be radiating good vibes. She could feel it from his expressions in the photos and this was proven so when they moved corresponding from the website to Whatsapp.

On one of these days their paths were destined to cross, but neither of them could really tell when. He was based elsewhere in Europe and with her in London this could prove to be tricky. Even when he did return to the UK, it would normally be to his hometown of Edinburgh, rather than to her neck of the woods. Lou had used up her holiday allowance and could take no more days for a while. (That wasn't necessarily completely accurate, as she always kept a few back for contingency in case there was something that came up with her children, but he didn't need to know that.)

And so, as was becoming the norm it seemed, Lou and Rob played the waiting game until the time was right, which turned out to be around ten weeks later. Rob had decided to move back to his homeland but would be taking a well-earned break and do some Greek island hopping first for a month. It was during this time that Lou felt she really got to know him. With more time on his hands and less distractions, his messaging became more frequent and all the more descriptive of his thoughts, feelings and experiences during his time out. The more Lou heard, the more she liked his gentle calm way about him.

When planning the next part of his own journey, Rob decided to take a detour to London ahead of commencing his new life back in Scotland. His sole purpose was to meet Lou and she couldn't help but feel flattered. Rob decided to fly back into her city and spend the weekend. This was all a bit risky Lou thought and made that very clear to him. "You're assuming that we click and will want to spend more than just an evening together. What if we don't? I hope you've got a plan b." But both of them knew that it was highly unlikely he would need one. Regardless, this was an entire weekend Rob was talking about and Lou's time without her children was supremely precious. She didn't want to commit just in case it didn't quite pan out as positively as they both were both hoping. "How about we meet after work Friday? Let's go for a drink and maybe some dinner. If all goes well then you can decide if you want to stay the night and then the weekend. I'm going to be in London any way and you might as well cancel any potential other plans for Saturday and Sunday. I very much doubt you'll

2

be seeing anyone else." Lou loved the confidence and imagined the message had been transmitted with that same cheeky smile she had seen in his pics.

Prior to his visit they had agreed that if there was the chemistry they anticipated, then they would visit one of the swinging clubs in the area. There were a few to choose from so they kept their options open until nearer the time. Meanwhile Lou made sure they had been accepted for their various memberships in advance. Lou had heard of a kinkier BDSM event on the Saturday night not far away and that could also be an option. Tickets were relatively cheap and Lou had bought two online just in case. If Rob turned out to be nothing like she thought, she'd drag someone else along to join her. She had plenty of other friends that would be up for a giggle and the tickets certainly wouldn't be wasted.

Rob's flight came into London City Airport at 12:30 but, much to her annoyance, Lou couldn't get away from her work any sooner that day. She would have to be hard at it in the office still while he sipped his cool beer in a roof top bar near Bank station. He'd brought the sunshine with him too and that made it all the more torturous for Lou as she sat in Canary Wharf wondering how the evening would develop.

Fortunately Lou was very busy, so the afternoon did pass relatively quickly, although not speedily enough! By 17:00 Lou couldn't contain her excitement any longer. She skipped down to the Docklands Light Railway (DLR) and was soon taken on the driver-less train to finally meet this very attractive Scotsman.

They were messaging throughout the 20-minute journey and to Lou's surprise, as she stepped off the

3

DLR, she suddenly felt a pang of nervousness. Lou wasn't exactly sure why. She felt like she knew him already after all, but the final hurdle still needed to be overcome. Wheeling her small trolley dolly to the lift for the bar, she entered and took a deep breath. 'Here we go!' she thought to herself. 'It's now or never.'

Rob had told her where he was sitting, when he enquired as to her arrival time and drink request. It was a table for two in the direct sunshine, which sounded perfect, and her gin and tonic was already waiting for her. (Oh, he was good!) He admitted he was super excited to finally meet her and she felt the same, albeit with a little trepidation.

He was easy to spot as she disembarked the lift. It was the back of him she saw first. He was wearing a blue cotton shirt, casual shorts and sandals. How very laid back indeed, and he certainly rocked this look. Lou came up close behind him and said, "Welcome to London young man. Fancy seeing you here!" She was right about the smile. It was quite sensational. He displayed it in all its glory as he stood up and gave her a massive hug. "I'm very pleased to be here Lou. Even more so now." Now they both beamed like Cheshire cats as they reflected on their respective catches. There was no disappointment on either side, and so the conversation, now in person at last, began to flow effortlessly.

They had a few drinks before deciding to move on to the hotel to 'dump their bags.' Given their previous messages and now their physical discussions, they both knew that entering a hotel room together and withdrawing themselves rapidly from it was likely to be increasingly problematic. With a few drinks inside them and the levels of excitement they were both sharing, a quick bag drop would be a challenge, which they accepted, knowing the risks! They both needed food, so it would be the right choice to make a quick dash in and then continue on to a restaurant elsewhere. Well, that was the plan any way.

It was only a short walk to the hotel and despite her heels Lou was quite keen on a stroll through the city. It had been a number of years since she had worked in this location, plus the sun was shining, so why not? They walked from Bank to Aldgate, with Lou pointing out gargoyles and describing various landmarks on route.

Twenty minutes later and they were checking in. This is where their levels of self-control were about to be tested, starting with the lift. Surprisingly, they both kept it together and flirted outrageously therein, but didn't once touch each other. Maybe they would pass this test after all and make it to the restaurant...

Or not? Once inside the room it was a whole different story. They joked about what a lovely couple they made and as if to prove it, stood in front of the mirror for confirmation. That was all it took. Rob stood tall behind Lou and nuzzled into her neck as they posed for an imaginary photo and with his arms now around her, it was just seconds before their tongues were clashing with great gusto. The passion had been building and was now at boiling point. There would be no return (and most definitely no restaurant, that was for sure)!

Rob spun Lou around so he could have full access to her mouth. The kissing was heated and their tongues were well matched, with saliva in abundance they continued their duel. "Ah fuck it! Come on then!" Lou expelled in sheer delight. She raised her dress over her head and slung it to the floor to reveal the black basque she had been saving for him all day. He was suitably impressed. "Well look at you," Rob said with delight: eyes sparkling and those pearly white teeth gleaming at her. He really did have an amazing mouth. She couldn't wait to see how it performed on her nether regions, and that didn't take too long to find out.

What Lou did discover about Rob was that he had a thing about saliva. He liked the way it formed chains between their mouths and from time to time he would draw back just to watch the display this moisture had created before them. This wasn't just between mouth and mouth, but with his mouth and her pussy, as well as her mouth and his penis. He really found it fascinating and it seemed that every wet connection brought its own visual delights for him, as well as sensual delights for them both.

Suffice to say that the months of waiting and building for this moment were well worth it and without disappointment. The next three hours consisted of them discovering more about each other than they'd only ever surmised in flirtatious chat before. He spent a lot of that time admiring her neatly shaved pussy and how each twist, turn, lick and lap of his tongue made her react, with numerous orgasms along the way. He was very talented here and his hunger for her was strong. It had been a few weeks since he was last with a woman, so the desire was pent up and eager to be released. Lucky Lou!

In return for his delicious feast on her pussy, Lou maintained eye contact throughout her devouring of his cock. There was definitely a sizzling connection between them: with both feeling almost like they had been lovers before (in a previous life perhaps), such was their knowing of what would hit the spot. Rob watched in anticipation as she slowly moved from thigh to groin and groin to other thigh as she dragged her tongue across, licking and nibbling all around his throbbing penis. He loved the teasing and growled from time to time before laughing. "Fuck yeah woman. I like that."

When she sensed he could endure no more teasing, she concentrated solely on his cock, which was certainly ready for her. Having discovered his saliva love, she made a point of drooling all over the tip and letting it run down his wanton shaft. His eyes revealed the excitement as much as his manhood did. They were radiating delight as Lou gradually took him hungrily. Slowly to begin, he could feel every tingly sensation of her mouth beginning to grip the sides as she slid up and down. "Oh yes!" Rob screamed out quite unexpectedly. This was proving quite the delight for them both, because Lou absolutely loved to watch the pleasure she was responsible for creating.

Rob was more than ready to penetrate her and given they were both super charged and most definitely wet, it only seemed right that she should climb aboard his delicious member, once a condom was firmly in place. Both of them had come prepared and they appreciated they would need to interrupt this steamy session before they could continue. ('That's a relief!' Lou thought. These situations could be tricky if the partner was reluctant to use protection - which for Lou would mean play stopped. It just wasn't worth the risk.) Rob reached into his bag and brought one out, slipped it on and they were ready to rock and roll. To her relief he hadn't lost any strength down there and he was once again pointing to the ceiling as Lou lowered herself down.

Purposely she did this very slowly and as Lou descended, she looked deep into his sparkly eyes. They were looking directly back at her as he grabbed her hands and their fingers entwined just as their bodies fused. "Wow!" Lou gasped but almost in a whisper. She really did feel they were locked as one. A pause of reflection and realisation of feelings and sensations shared was taken before they continued. This was a moment to savour. Something very special was taking place here and it was one to cherish...

Before the frantic, rough, hard, thrashing fucking began and wouldn't relent until they became so fatigued and famished that they had to break away from each other to nourish their other bodily needs. They had pretty much covered at least one circuit of the hotel room, using every surface possible; leaving sweaty hand, feet, bum and boob prints on mirrors and glass, as they discovered new vantage points and explored different positions. 'Holy Moly, Macaroni, that was awesome,' Lou thought as they finally made their way to the shower. (Fuck knew where that expression had come from!) This had been far better than she had imagined it would be.

Time had sped past and they were way beyond regular eating hours. Restaurants outside of the hotel were packing up as they ventured out into the street and in search of food. Another budget hotel close by was still serving food and Lou had tried their pizzas before. They were positively mediocre but right now they'd taste absolutely divine, so that's where they headed. They sat inside and another large gin and tonic accompanied their food; both went down a treat. They had certainly earned it! Their conversations now were more along the lines of contemplation and reminiscing. What an incredible evening they'd had (so far). "So did I pass?" he asked her with an impish smile on his face. "Do I get to spend more time with you Ms. Busy Lou?" 'Fuck yeah,' Lou thought to herself. She knew this definitely would be a whole weekender with Rob and not just the Friday night. He was way too good to let go now, particularly when she had another potential night (maybe two) with his adorable and incredibly sexy self. "Yes, you did all right!" she mocked, but they both knew it had been a remarkably hot session.

Once their energy reserves were restocked, they made their way back to the hotel and it wasn't long before they started over again. It was far more sensual this time and tender now that they were properly acquainted. Afterwards Lou did actually fall asleep in his arms, which was very unusual for her. Normally she would break away and sleep on her side, but the events of the evening and the connection she felt made it easy to doze off happily in his embrace.

The entire weekend was fun-filled and exciting. Gay Pride was on in London and the streets were buzzing with colour and frivolity. The pair, arm in arm and suitably filled following a hearty breakfast in Aldgate, made their way to Soho. They wandered along in the sunshine, taking in all the celebratory sights on show rather than the usual tourist attractions. Plotting up in a bar, they drank, chatted and people-watched as the many exhibitionists sauntered past on their way to the parade or to meet with friends. They found it entertaining to watch such a glorious array of people all buzzing around in a world of their own.

After a few drinks, this new and rather natural twosome made their way to Regent Street where the floats had begun to slowly pour their way along the crowd-filled pavements. It was quite a spectacle, made all the more enjoyable by the blistering sunshine, which was always a welcomed surprise in London! Those glamorous outfits must have been sweltering to wear and some make up had begun to look a little sweaty on some of those glammed up for the event.

Rob and Lou decided to head back to the hotel. They were feeling hot too but in a different way. Their evening event was beckoning and a little pre-night action was definitely on the cards before they went out. It would be the warm up to whatever decadence they ended up partaking in later.

Lou took great delight in showing Rob the various outfits she had brought along for tonight's adventure. He liked the leather choice. There was very little of it: a leather leotard with metal chains across the breasts. And there was that instant beaming smile. It was the winner. She covered it with a full-length dress, with side splits to the hips and five-inch stilettos. Lou felt sexy for him and couldn't wait to be on show on his arm and later in more compromising positions.

Parading around in her various outfits, Lou knew this would be enough to get them both in the mood. Once the outfit decision was made, she slipped out of it so it wouldn't get messy for later. There would be plenty of time to soil it at the event. For now, there was a rather ravenous appetite or two that needed to be satisfied, and they had plenty of time ahead of going out. It would have been rude not to!

A cramped shower later proved that it was way more practical to be in there one at a time. Rob volunteered to exit it first, to allow her to wash her hair. This gave Lou the opportunity to relax a little before psyching herself up for the next section of this adventurous weekend.

There was no rush to get going. Lou took her time making herself beautiful and Rob was happy enough just to watch. Like most men, the period he took was minimal but he was content and looking rather chilled out on the bed waiting for her. Lou applied her makeup and gave him a few cheeky smiles in the mirror. This pair of such recent strangers were so much more relaxed now in each other's company, like they been lovers for years.

When the time came nearer to depart, they toyed with going to the swinging club less than five minutes' walk away. It had been an option for this evening, but Lou felt obliged to try the other event, particularly as she had already purchased the tickets. If they found this BDSM night wasn't their cup of tea, they could always change location later.

Their cab dropped them at the door of an archway underneath the Liverpool Street railway line in the Bethnal Green area. It was a cobbled street, which was no doubt steeped in history, but not particularly practical for Lou's heels! She showed her phone's online tickets at the makeshift reception area and they made their way inside. This is where the night took a strange turn for the inquisitive couple. Just about everything seemed to be black: the decor, the props, the outfits and the mood too. It was empty inside the venue, possibly because many of the usual clientele were at Pride parties elsewhere, which were no doubt heaving. Upon reflection, it wasn't the best night to try somewhere new, Lou thought to herself.

As it was their first time here, they accepted the offer of the tour, but this did nothing to ease their unrest. They didn't feel at all comfortable, although it was interesting all the same. Those who were assembled seemed quite cliquey and were not inviting these newbies into their fold. Rob bought them both a drink, which they consumed rather rapidly, probably because they were served in such small plastic glasses. It all felt a bit shabby really.

A second drink in and the only brightly dressed person in the room approached them from the other side of this small main room. "Hello. I'm Brian. I'm 64 you know. You'd never guess it, would you?" Well the honest answer was of course no. He looked at least that and more, but neither of them was going to tell him, and so the awkwardness began.

Brian was very keen to introduce them to 'Snacks' who was a miniature Scooby Doo toy who was perched hanging out of the small rucksack on Brian's back. "He goes everywhere with me," he joyfully told them. 'Oh boy,' Lou thought. It was hard enough to concentrate on what they were being told without looking directly at Brian's toothless mouth. Well having said that, he did have two teeth on show on the bottom row. It was impossible to see any on the top. "He's my best friend. He was with me every step of the way when I had throat cancer." Well that hit a nerve and couldn't be ignored. They offered their sympathies but Brian assured them he had been given the all clear and was thrilled to have overcome this awful disease. "Oh that's great news," Lou congratulated him. "Well done you for beating the bastard." Brian was all smiles. He even gave them a twirl that was partly to show Snacks to them but also to reveal more of his outfit. It was a pink fairy costume with netting underneath that made the skirt flare outwards as he spun. "Beautiful," Rob stated, looking ever more uncomfortable the more the conversation continued.

Before Brian launched into any more of his self-revelations, Lou said, "I'm just popping to the toilet," as she walked off, leaving Rob with a pained look on his face of 'please don't leave me.' But Lou had a cunning plan which she needed to execute away from the men. In the loo, she ordered an Uber as she hovered over the toilet and did a wee. She was good at multi-tasking! Fortunately it was just minutes away and they could escape this crazy place.

Coming back into the room she thought of a way to separate them without being rude to Brian. "Come on Rob, let's have a cigarette outside." Knowing full well that like herself, Rob didn't smoke, she was sure this would split them up, but alas it was foiled. "Ah, hang on. I'll come out the back there and have one with you," Brian stated. Lou was flabbergasted. Oh come on: surely not? This man had survived throat cancer. Why would he want to join them? "It's ok Brian," she retorted immediately. "We're going out the front!" With that, she scooped Rob's arm in hers and marched him to the exit, leaving Brian with a somewhat shocked look on his face. It was similar to the expression Rob now displayed, as he had no idea what was going on until he got outside. "Our Uber is on its way. Let's get the hell out of here," Lou reassured him. Pure relief engulfed his face. "Thank fuck for that! I didn't know how much more of that I could have taken."

The cab ride was full of laughter. What a brilliant escape! Their adventure was now heading back towards Aldgate for attempt number two at a naughty night out. Thankfully it was more successful than the first. Perhaps they should have just gone there in the first place? Lou had always experienced a good night there before. On the other hand, they would never have met Brian or Snacks and shared that rather odd experience. It certainly gave the evening a twist and the pair of them a few laughs!

The cab took them directly to the club that was just minutes from where they were staying. Fortunately the events of the night now took a more fruitful turn. As they had found themselves so totally into each other, they just played as a pair: not inviting anyone else to join them, nor were they tempted to play outside of their newly found desire. It proved to be a much better evening than what they envisaged at their earlier aborted experience.

When they returned to the hotel, Rob unexpectedly surprised Lou with a gift he'd bought her at one of his Greek island hops. It was a delicate silver bracelet, which she was overwhelmed with. It was just her style. How could he have known? Rob revealed he had undertaken some investigative work and seen in photos online the sort of jewellery Lou wore. 'How thoughtful was this man?' Lou contemplated. He said he had chosen it carefully and knew she would like it. He was right too. Well he was proving he really was quite a gem! He did up the clasp on her wrist and it looked perfect. It sat well with the others she already adorned and were similar in design. Lou thanked him in her own special way and

14

afterwards they both went to sleep incredibly smiley, and slept like logs! It had been a very long and exhausting day, but so much fun too.

The next morning this loved up pair woke up horny. Seems this was the norm for them both. It didn't matter how much sex they had already: the more you have, the more you want. Now was no different and the next hour and half was spent interlocked in various ways before they went out for a café breakfast. They had certainly earned the nourishment given how many calories they had just burnt off! They then decided to take a leisurely mooch up and down the ever funky Sunday Brick Lane. It was refreshing not to have to rush anywhere and just to enjoy the time they had together.

Rob was gob-smacked to hear Lou reveal later that she had planned to stay over Sunday night too. Lou had kept that one up her sleeve, just in case she felt she'd outstayed her welcome, or it became dull. Luckily neither of those was felt and she took great delight in telling him the good news. The surprise went down a treat. Another whole night together - fantastic! Lou would make her way directly to work in the morning, and just so happened to have packed work clothes in that trolley dolly too: ever prepared eh? Well, you just never knew how these things would pan out. Lou was resourceful and knew it was always good to have options. The last thing she would have wanted is to have spent more time with this delicious man and not been able to. That would have been a tragic waste!

The pair treated themselves to a delicious pub roast nearby before retiring to their room and having some more fun, once the food had gone down. There was little energy left in the room once they finally dropped off to sleep, although they did muster just a little bit up in the morning before she departed for work.

Lou had a huge smile on her face as she wheeled her case onto the Tube. They had shared a delicious hug and lots of kisses before she left. Neither of them really wanted this adventure to come to an end. It had been surprisingly difficult to finally let him go as she walked away. However, it was inevitable, just as work was, and he had a plane to catch to Edinburgh. Lou spent a moment in reflection on the journey to the office: what a brilliant experience it had been. Here were two people who had never physically met, who had such an electric connection. They had managed to carry off spending three nights together like long established lovers and had a magical adventure. It was certainly one to remember and definitely to repeat again.

Chapter 2 - Cough please

Lou and Ross had many a naughty adventure during work time and looking back, she did wonder how on earth they got away with it? Lou would never dream of being that cheeky now. It was risking her career as well as Ross's marriage; the latter of which was not her concern. She took no responsibility for his misdemeanors.

They shared many role-play scenarios in London and on business trips and they both took the preparation very seriously. It all added to the anticipation for the receiver as well as the excitement for the creator. On this occasion it was Lou's turn to orchestrate the situation, which comprised of a hotel rendezvous where she would be first to arrive. This would allow her to set the scene for his impending delight.

Lou had thought this one through in great detail and she arrived with a bag of tricks at the ready. Inside was her purposely cheap-looking nurse's outfit, complete with red cross-adorned headband, plastic stethoscope and clipboard. The white suspender belt, fishnet stockings and blood red patent stilettos made the outfit complete. (They reminded Lou of her grammar school teacher who had explained why such material was not allowed: the shine would reflect a girl's underwear! This certainly would not have mattered in this scenario, not that Lou ever believed there was any truth in that statement!)

Lou lowered the flimsy, somewhat rickety zip to just below her ribcage so the outline of her breasts could clearly be seen. She swept her brown hair up into a bun and adorned a pair of fake spectacles. She was ready for his arrival.

Ross was instructed to knock at the door before he entered the 'waiting room'. It was time for his annual well-man check-up. "Come in," Lou acknowledged and in he walked. Ross looked at Lou in disbelief as he placed his coat and bag on the dressing table. "And you are Mr. Smith: is that correct?" Lou asked. Almost sheepishly Ross replied, "Yes, I'm Ross Smith." Lou ticked off his preprinted name on her paperwork. She continued with, "I just need to confirm your date of birth?" Ross happily gave the details, which Lou would never have known were correct or not, but that was unimportant. She directed him to the chair. "That's marvelous thank you. Do please take a seat Mr. Smith. I won't keep you waiting."

Ross adjusted himself as he sat down. Lou could tell he was a little nervous and inside she just wanted to give him a big hug, but that wasn't part of this role-play. Surprisingly, she didn't feel the urge to burst into giggles, which she had half anticipated and that in itself was a relief. It would have totally killed the moment.

"Now Mr. Smith, it has been over a year since your last well-man assessment. Have you had any issues you would like to discuss before we get started?" Ross looked at her with bewilderment and wonder. She could tell he was impressed with her attention to detail. "No, nothing sinister. I feel as fit as a fiddle, but it's always good to be sure." Lou was pleased he was acclimatising now. She found it hard to resist giving a double-entendre and retorted with "Oh it's always good... to be sure." It was a play on words, with deliberate pause, that amused her as she her perused her clipboard. There were a number of preprinted questions ready to be answered. She had done her homework and wanted this session to have the structure it deserved.

"If you would care to remove your clothes Mr. Smith? There is a dressing gown just there you can put on." Lou walked to the other side of the room and turned her back to give him some privacy. Obviously this was all part of the act. They had both seen each other naked enough times not to feel uncomfortable. From time to time she looked up over her glasses to watch him remove the garments. When he 'caught her looking', she pretended to act childishly embarrassed and quickly dropped her gaze back at the clipboard.

With the white toweling robe in place, very loosely tied, Ross sat back down and her comprehensive assessment began. The questions were standard, asking about age, type of job he performed, number of gym visits per week, foods eaten, etc. "I need to ask you to cough Mr. Smith, for which you will have to stand up." 'Oh yeah,' he thought. 'Here we go...'" And he was right. This is where it was going to start getting even more interesting.

"Please stand with your legs a shoulder width apart, as I cup my hand under your scrotum." Ross was happy to follow her lead. He coughed as instructed and she gently caressed his ball sack. "Thank you Mr. Smith. That was good, but we'll need to do it once more please, just to make sure." Ross wasn't entirely clear what she needed to

19

be sure of exactly (and neither did Lou, to be fair) but he complied willingly as she grabbed them a little harder and then nodded to him. "Oh that's much better. Thank you. You may take a seat once more." Ross was as bemused as she was and very happy to continue with this charade.

As Ross sat down, Lou informed him that he would be having a rectal examination next and he would need to lay on the bed on his side, with knees raised towards his chest. To be honest, she hadn't really thought this part through. Should he be on his side? Would that allow better access to his back passage? Or would it be simpler if he were on his front with his bum up in the air? This may have to be a process of elimination, but at least he was an eager participant in her experimentation and they could learn together!

Lou could clearly see Ross's growing erection poking through his robe and she knew that he would never have been able to lie down on his front if she had asked that of him. Lou pointed to the bed and said, "When you are ready Mr. Smith: if you could please lift up your robe, just to your waist to allow easier access?" Ross followed her instruction and noticed the tube of lubricant on the side, placed next to some latex gloves. A wave of relief clearly washed over him. Lou wondered if he thought she would do this dry or at best with saliva? Fortunately for him, she had thought of everything and not left it like most men Lou had encountered (who liked the 'bum sex'), to spit on their hands, smother the orifice and hope that was enough! In her own experience, Lou found it never was quite enough and lubricant was way more comfortable!

Somewhat overly dramatically, Lou put on the clear latex gloves for him to see. (She reminded herself of a Customs and Excise officer about to start an internal inspection.) Next she opened the 'lube' and very generously distributed it over her hands and across his anus. She lent over to his right ear and said in an especially soft whisper, "I will be very gentle with you Mr. Smith," as she began to caress his very sensitive bottom. Slipping up and down the crack, Lou rubbed her fingers ever closer to the opening. She noticed Ross's breathing become deeper as she continued the motion. He was easing into the rhythm, as the tip of her index finger sympathetically penetrated the entrance and he gasped ever so slightly. She knew him well enough to know how much he had wanted this to happen and that his wife would never dream of performing such an allegedly 'disgusting' act on him. However, Lou was only too happy to make this a reality for him. After all, she had previously let him into her own anal passage when he had earned 'privileged access' *(readers refer to Vanilla Extract for a definition),* so only fair now to do the same to him.

Ross was relaxing more now in order to control the sensations. The concentration had allowed his deep breathing to become more regulated and he was craving further stimulation. "How does that feel Mr. Smith? I know these examinations can be a little undignified, but they are essential. Are you ready for me to conduct the full internal examination now?" Ross nodded and whilst almost bursting with anticipation, he raised his head to look directly at her. "Yes please nurse. Do go ahead." Lou was surprised by his calm and calculated response. He

21

was doing very well to maintain this air when she knew inside he was gagging for more.

This gave Lou the opportunity to ask Ross to change position. Whilst she had tried slipping her finger in his wanton orifice, she found his other buttock was getting in the way. With gravity pulling it downwards upon the lower one, it was squashing the opening closed and thereby obstructing exactly where she needed to be driving her moistened digit. Not letting this faze her, she said, "Mr Smith: would you mind just popping yourself up onto your knees, with your bottom raised upwards in the air? It will be more comfortable for you." Ross did as he was asked and Lou was pleased with the result. It would be much more accessible in this position.

With more lube applied, she began to gradually enter his arse. Knowing how uncomfortable this could be from her own experiences, Lou was very delicate with Ross - possibly a little too much. Once her finger was fully inside, she began to move it up and down creating a rhythm that increased in speed and depth ever so slightly. Lou had looked up prostrate milking the week before and was keen to give it a go. Described as a 'come here' motion, Lou adopted this technique and it seemed to be doing the trick, but she wanted to be sure. It was her first time after all and she was looking for some reassurance that she was doing it right. "I hope that's not too uncomfortable for you Mr. Smith?" Ross nodded his head and smiled back at her. No words were required as his face displayed all the confirmation she needed. 'Oh he is doing just fine,' Lou thought. He had initially drawn a sharp intake of breath as it became more vigorous, but he soon began to unwind and enjoy the new sensations that he too was experiencing for the first time.

"Oh Lou, that's mad. I can't describe it… It feels really odd, but it's truly awesome at the same time." To add to the sensory overload, Lou gently placed her left hand on his bulging penis. He wasn't expecting it and quivered as she began to rub it at the same time as she proceeded to milk him. "Fuck Lou, it's fucking amazing. I'm tingly all over… Shit Lou, I'm so close. Believe me, I'm fighting this. I really am, but it just feels too good. I don't want to come yet, but I really don't know how long I can hold out here." Lou was quite pleased with herself and of course she wanted him to enjoy this moment, but selfishly she didn't really want him to come – not just yet any way. But Lou was a realist and she could tell she was losing this battle, well, she guessed it was winning in some respects. At least she knew she had got it right, judging by his reactions!

Lou increased the speed of her index finger 'come on' motion and the wanking of his cock with her other hand. She could feel his body begin to tense. "Fuck Lou I'm gonna come. I can't hold back any longer." The fight was over and there was no time elapse before he did exactly that. It was big. It was intense, but much to their surprise, whilst his body displayed all the signs of orgasm, there was no spunk to show for it. He convulsed in ecstasy and was jerking around all over the place, as was usual and he most definitely came, but there was not a drop of sperm anywhere. Both Lou and Ross looked at each other in dismay. Neither of them could quite believe it. He had just experienced his first dry ejaculation. Well that was certainly different!

Lou ever so slowly removed her finger from his bum. This was important, as she knew first hand, and meant his innards would be less traumatised than if she'd whipped it out speedily! Ross's body was still shaking as she did. She took her time to ensure he was as comfortable as possible as she rolled the glove inside out and threw it in the bin. Then Lou went into the bathroom and washed her hands. At the same time, much like any usual euphoria moment, Ross took a while to recover after coming and lay on the bed gazing up at the ceiling contemplating what had just happened. It was quite a surreal experience: far more so than he had imagined for this afternoon!

Lou jumped on the bed with him. "How are you feeling Mr. Smith?" She joked. He was smiling now with a gooey post-cum look on his face. In a sultry tone said, "Oh I'm feeling goooooood, but I really do need a wee! I have absolutely no idea what my body is doing right now. It's in a state of shock. It's all over the place. What did you do to me?" Ross made his way to the bathroom and after a while of apparent confusion, given his laughs, sighs and commentary from the toilet seat, he had managed to sort himself out and his body was becoming more of its usual familiar self.

With rather a healthy glow to his cheeks, Ross joined her in the bedroom. He had expected her to be waiting for him on the bed, but instead she had placed herself upon the chair. He had to double take as he located her. "Come here Mr. Smith. I haven't quite finished your assessment just yet." Ross's eyes lit up as he walked over to her. "Yes nurse," he mused. She opened her legs where she sat. "There is one more test we need to complete. I need to check how good your tongue reflexes are working today. Please kneel down just here." He was entirely compliant as he took up the position before her and began to demonstrate his oral skills. Lou shuffled closer to the edge of the chair and spread her legs wider to give further access to her freshly waxed pussy. This was just what she needed now, having focused all her attention on him in this session. It was time for her to receive some of the good stuff. After all, Lou had 'worked' so very well to deserve it and she was already dribbling on the seat with excitement before he even began.

On this occasion it was relatively easy for Ross to make Lou come, given how incredibly charged she was from the scenario she had created and rather excellently delivered. It was not unusual with him (and many others) that Lou would have to play with her own clit to come, but today that was totally unnecessary. It was not long after unzipping her purposely cheap nurse outfit and nibbling her breasts whilst finger fucking her, that the explosion quickly arrived.

It was Lou's turn to feel the relief now and she enjoyed every current that ran through her body. 'Damn that was good,' she happily thought, but this party wasn't over yet. She wanted at least two more before the time came for them to fuck, which they went on to do in real style. This was a build up for them both and the only way to deal with it in true Lou fashion, was to pound each other silly, in every position, in every part of the bedroom. They certainly made every penny of that hotel day rate charge count, as they pumped their afternoon away. They were both covered in sweat and each other's juices as his final crescendo beckoned. Lou had already come a number of times and it was now a case of him needing to climax before they both grew too sore. "Yes Lou, I'm gonna come." They switched positions as she climbed down from onboard his cock and knelt on the bed below his straddled legs. Lou enjoyed giving oral pleasure, so she was only too pleased to go to work on his scrotum and penis. Given his 'privileged access,' Lou indicated that she would take his load in her mouth. She wondered if it would be another dry one, but had a funny feeling that would be somewhat unlikely, and she was correct.

The thick, hot, sticky liquid filled her mouth. She could feel it was gloopy and salty and was keen to get it down before she gagged. It worked. All evidence was now gone as she swallowed it quickly. Lou knew he would be keen to taste his come, so she made her way to the top of the bed and kissed him deeply straight afterwards. It was something he enjoyed and she was happy to share it with him. Well if she had tasted it, then why shouldn't he? She'd sampled her own juices plenty of times! He shared the remnants of his own flavour before they pulled apart. It was time for them both to catch their breaths and reflect on their rather crazy few hours together before jumping in the shower.

Fortunately neither of them had to go back to the office. No one would be any the wiser of their afternoon sex-scapade. It was now safely locked away in the naughty chest of shared treasure, along with many other sexy interludes. Lou wondered where their next one would take place: here, Sydney, Hong Kong? Who knew, but they both knew for certain that it would be a whole lot of fun. It always was!

Chapter 3 - Crossing the line

It had been just under a year since the 'Flavas' had partied together and finally they were all free on this particular Friday night. *(The Flavas are a group of variously aged ladies who liked to party and swing together. They first met in Vanilla Extract.)* Separate variations of groupings had taken place since their last planned encounter: when two of them went for dinner in Covent Garden, the same two partied at a new event in south London and three of them randomly crossed paths by accident at a party. However, this was the first time all four of them were actually available and had arranged to spend a naughty night out together.

Interestingly the location most convenient for their reunion was the very place they had met, some three years earlier, at this beautiful house near St. Albans. It was quite unbelievable to think it had been that long, so it would be a good place to both reminisce and catch up on what everyone had been up to.

Two of the group had arranged to stay in the local pub, whilst one lived locally and Lou was quite happy to drive home. She had been stranded once at that very same pub, sitting in a bath questioning what on earth she was doing with her life, and she didn't particularly want a repeat of that tonight. By having her car to hand, she knew there was nothing to stop her from making a sober departure later at whatever time she chose.

Lou parked in the grounds of the party and meandered from the back of the property to the front door, where the lovely homeowner, with whom she'd built up a friendship previously, greeted her with open arms. They were both pleased to see each other, as it had been a while, and they nattered heartily until they were interrupted by the arrival of other partygoers. Lou made her apologies and went inside. Rebecca was already in the kitchen with her 'number three' fuck buddy, as in he was her third best at the time. Sabrina was with them both and Lucy was expected within the next 20 minutes. It was like old times and immediately they slipped back into it.

The three ladies chatted about just about everything they could cram in: outfits, men, children, parties, food and drink, with Rebecca's partner looking a little lost at times. About half an hour later, Lucy joined them with a whole new drama to explain. She told them how the journey had been horrendous, although the young stallion that accompanied her had certainly made up for it! She staggered into the room, bouncing off him and the walls, and it was clear the two of them had started their partying way before they arrived here.

With the banter now in full swing, it was comforting for Lou to have like-minded people around. For a while now she had felt a little out on a limb with this lifestyle she was living out. She was going back around the loop of 'is this it?' It was a regular cycle of enjoying the swinging scene to a point of saturation and not just on the bodily juices variety. Lou would get bored of the hedonism in favour of a steady (dare I say 'vanilla') connection and wondered if a little more stability was in order? Equally, however, in the relationships she had since her divorce, she soon found they became tiresome too. Lou had even tried a combination of the too, with a swinging partnership, and the intention to play as a couple, but that had not gone according to plan when he proved he wanted her just for himself.

Tonight they would let their hair down and party without inhibition. Time was ticking on and whilst they were amusing each other, they couldn't help but notice the place wasn't filling up. In fact, rather disappointingly, it was fairly empty. This was not boding well for their intended night of decadence. The drinkers continued to fuel their fun, but Lou was growing concerned that this would be a wash out. They would wait till the pubs turned out and see if the numbers increased as a result. That would be the only way this party would be salvaged, otherwise Lou would be back on the M25 earlier than anticipated.

Lou's instincts were right and a few more single guys did show up and added to the numbers, but sadly not much to the quality! However, one did catch Lou's eye. He was quite short at around 5' 7" and slight, but he had a very cute face and glistening eyes. He had a bit of a greying quiff going on with his hair and a tidy goatie beard. It wasn't long before they struck up a conversation and upon remarking about his accent, Lou learned that he was Lee from Leeds and came from close to where her daughter had just finished university. He was quite a cheeky chap and she liked that. It made up for his scruffy appearance, which he blamed on going straight to the pub from work and then onto the party afterwards. 'It was just as well he had the gift of the gab' Lou thought.

Tonight found the Flavas more subdued than previous

groupings. This was due to there being less people to play with for starters, but perhaps they had grown up a little more now; well Lou felt she had at least? Lucy and her young man had decided the party wasn't going to pick up, so they chose to go back to their hotel and continue there instead. Lou couldn't help but feel Lucy was leaving on his instruction rather than by choice, but she put up no fight and even gave them all a slobbery kiss before they departed. She asked Lou if she wanted to join them but with her car parked here, Lou was reluctant to go to a different location in the opposite direction to her home. She could also tell how pissed the two of them were and she wasn't particularly keen on trying to catch up, nor be their taxi service.

As the night went on, it was clear Lee and Lou would be taking this further. The flirting had not ebbed from the moment they began speaking and it wasn't long before they took themselves upstairs to the same room where the Flavas had put on quite a show when they first met. It had been much more of an orgy on that occasion, with a school disco theme, and they had left the location saturated all over. They had even taken a countless number of photographs of the action they enjoyed as a group, which is usually a taboo at such events. However, they were careful to ensure no one else was in the pictures: just themselves in their rampant soiree. (To protect people's privacy, taking pictures is forbidden, but the Flavas had been reckless and wild that night, blatantly taking no notice of the rules back then.) No one actually challenged them to stop, so they happily snapped away.

In the room now were Rebecca and her 'friend', Lou and Lee and another couple. The beds were set up differently and on opposite sides instead of all joined, as they had been the last time they had wrecked this room. This made the couplings separate rather than interlocked and together. Lou didn't mind this arrangement and gave her focus only to Lee. Even when the door opened for others to join them, she was adamant that they didn't. This was mainly because she had scanned the other attendees and there was no one else she wanted to join their private party. Snobby as that sounded, Lou was particular about what she did and didn't like, and she'd already carried out her quality assurance review downstairs. The door was definitely to stay shut!

It wasn't long before Rebecca and her man were hard at it. She was a moaner and a very loud one at that. It made Lou smile. It had been a long time since she'd heard her at full pelt and she'd forgotten just how vocal she became! Lee was quite distracted and asked Lou if her friend was ok, which she certainly was and by no means was being murdered, which was an easy misconception given her dulcet tones!

The other couple was very quiet by comparison and you hardly knew they were there. As there seemed to be no interaction required by any of them, Lou and Lee began to get to know each other a little more intimately now and were soon lost in each other to take much notice of those around them.

The exploration was fun, as it always was with a stranger, and the pair took it in turns to uncover what made the other one flutter, sigh, gasp and lick their lips. It was the best pairing Lou could have hoped for this evening, with the night earlier looking like disappointment was inevitable. Now it was salvaged and proving to be much more exciting than she had initially thought.

Suddenly there was some movement close by. Rebecca and her partner had fulfilled their desires for the night and were now leaving. Lou waved between her legs in the air as they departed and Lee continued to slide his cock in and out as she did. Nothing was going to interrupt his flow.

At some stage the other couple must have left too, but it went unnoticed as the pair tried different positions on and around the bed. Lou remembered the balcony outside this room and when they both became incredibly hot, she opened the door up out to it. The Flavas had enjoyed putting on quite a show there, along with two strapping men. She resumed the position she had held years before, when Andy the Impaler had pounded her against it overlooking other party guests below them. This time it was Lee and it was pitch black with no one else watching, but it was enough to cool them both down before going back into their now private bedroom.

It was almost two hours and four condoms later before the couple finally relented and let their bodies get some rest. Despite not having a drink and being able to drive, the homeowners offered up the bedrooms for guests to sleep and that's exactly what they needed now. Lou almost kicked herself. She could have had a drink after all, but it wasn't the end of the world. It had been a good night and now time to get some shut-eye.

When she woke some six hours later, Lee was still fast asleep. He wasn't snoring but breathing deeply and she sent a quick message to her Flavas and Unicorns friendship groups. "I think I may have killed some guy

32

called Lee," she joked and received quite a few funny responses from her girlfriends. It was something they often shared after such quests.

Lou gathered her bits together, which didn't consist of much: knickers, bra, clothes, shoes and clutch bag with keys. Her jacket she had left in the car, however there was no mistaking how her neighbours would perceive this return home, should she bump into any of them. This didn't bother her in the slightest. They could think what they liked. Lou was living her life to the full and pondered on the "here for a good time, not a long time" or whatever that saying was.

Lee was stirring. "Morning you. I'm going to make a move. Do you need a lift?" she asked. He had told her the night before that he had his son on the Saturday, so he would have to be 'with it' before 10am. Fortunately it was only 8.30am, so he had plenty of time. "You're alright pet. I can walk from here." 'Fair enough,' Lou thought, 'even better,' she could make her way directly home. They exchanged numbers and said they'd meet up in the following week.

Surprisingly for Lou, they did continue their banter all over the weekend. She had half expected it to be a fuck that wouldn't have amounted to much more, but actually Lee was pretty funny and she liked his outlook on life. Maybe they would meet midweek as they had planned after all, rather than just saying it without ever meaning it to progress. Lou had come a long way from previous encounters following her divorce, where she hadn't even asked for their number, or their name for that matter. When she thought that neither of them was really interested in the other person, and mutual using had just occurred, she wasn't likely to call them and they weren't like to call her either, so what was the point of the pretense? Enjoy the sex: have the fun and then leave it there. Why bother expecting anything else from that person? It had been cut and dried for Lou and very simplistic. Why complicate it by adding emotion? It was a concept very few men understood from a woman, despite acting exactly the same way towards women themselves.

It was actually only two days after they first met that their paths crossed once more. Lee had told her his son was going home on the Sunday afternoon and he was free that evening. Being childfree that weekend herself Lou was also at a loose end and was available to meet. Dinner was arranged close to Lee's house and she was welcome to stay, which she undoubtedly would.

Lee explained that he had a very large dog and asked Lou if that would be an issue? To be honest, Lou wasn't really a 'dog person' but could tolerate the well behaved and non-slobbery, non-begging varieties. By the sounds of it, this German Shepherd was Lee's best friend and Lou wondered if it would get jealous of Lee's new female 'friend'. Lee confirmed he was a good dog and Lou would be very welcomed by them both, which was a relief to her.

The plans were set and worryingly, Lee said he would have to have a good tidy up of his house before she arrived. It had apparently been a while since he had 'entertained' at home. Lou jokingly said not to go to any trouble, but in her mind she was hoping this meant he would make sure there were no dog hairs all over the place to stick to her clothes! Minor alarm bells were going off at this point in Lou's mind and she really should have taken more notice. Her intuition was to be trusted, as she had learned the hard way before.

Sunday afternoon soon came around and given their weekend of shared messages to date, Lou was quite excited to see Lee once more. The pub he'd nominated was a short stroll from his house, which was in a country lane near Radlett. Lou would park at his and then they would take a walk up the lane for their dinner and drinks.

Lou decided on a casual look for this evening, given he had first seen her in her party clothes of a figure-hugging dress and heels. Tonight would be more subdued given it was a Sunday night in the local with any other 'vanillas' who were out for the evening. Tight dark navy jeans, peep-toe heels and a smart but relaxed crotchet top was the order for the evening's attire. It ticked the 'casual but classy' look she was going for.

The satnav took her straight past his house and when she messaged to say she was possibly lost, he said he would come out and wave her down. This worked a treat and fortunately didn't end up with her running him over or a trip to Accident and Emergency – always a bonus!

Lou parked her car on his drive and after grabbing a quick peck on the cheek, decided to head straight up to the pub for food. It was literally five minutes away and before they knew it, a roast dinner each was delivered to their table. Lou was pleased that the portions were not overly generous, as she didn't want to feel bloated for afterwards. The stroll back helped settle the food before they arrived back at his house. Lee went in first and let his dog out into the back garden, which was thoughtful of him. He said 'Roger' would get over-excited, so it would be best if he were let out instead.

Despite leaving his dog in the garden, what hit Lou first when she went into Lee's house, was the overwhelming smell of his canine companion. Whilst he had tried to disguise it with liberal sprays of Fabreze, by the counteracting aroma she could detect, it didn't touch the sides. There was no getting away from it, which was not pleasant in the slightest, which was a shame. Lee was amusing, had a good personality and had actually gone to a lot of trouble. She could see there were no hairs on the furniture, so he had cleaned as promised. Lou decided to try to bear it rather than spoil her night, but she certainly would not be sleeping here. She could feel the film of grime building up on her skin already. Thank goodness she'd only had one drink at the pub and could drive home later!

Lee offered her a drink as she sat on the sofa and cheekily, given the mental calculations and swift decision-making, Lou asked for a coffee. He looked a little surprised but happily accommodated her request. It wasn't a particularly good coffee either but it meant her gin and tonic was more diluted now, which gave her some comfort for the impending departure after their interactions.

They began to kiss in the living room and it was starting to get rather heated between them. Being ever more assisting, Lee asked if she wanted to go up to the bedroom, where they could relax more. Lou was happy with that suggestion and they made their way upstairs.

In Lee's bedroom, on the edge of the bed, they continued getting reacquainted, but something was troubling Lou. Directly opposite where they were sitting, the wardrobe door was just slightly ajar. It was only a small gap, say 2cm, but something about it didn't feel right. Her 'spidey senses' were in alarm. For all Lou knew, Lee had a camera in there and was about to film their naughty encounter. She had to say something. "Do you mind if we shut that door?" He looked puzzled. The bedroom door was already shut. "No, that door," she said as she pointed to the wardrobe. Lee laughed. "It's ok Lou. Don't be scared. There's no monster in there to gobble you up." It was Lou's turn to joke now. "Oh it's not a monster that worries me. It's more like if you're recording us." He looked at her in disbelief, shook his head, but did get up quickly and shut the door.

They had sex. It was on the cards and they both knew it. The dinner and chat was a formality really, but that's not to say it wasn't a laugh. It was a good forerunner to the carnal act that followed and was enjoyed. It wasn't the best sex she'd had, but it served its purpose. Once they had both 'filled their boots' Lou broke the news that she would be heading home. She made some excuse about not being able to sleep in other people's houses, just as she hadn't done particularly well when they first met. She would be hitting the motorway home instead and while Lee was openly disappointed, he said he understood. Despite the late hour, she was pleased to be going home so she could have a good shower. Lou was desperate to get the residue off her skin: not just bodily fluids but the lingering stench of dog, which felt like a film of dirt all over her. She couldn't wait to wash it off.

Lou climbed into her own bed at almost 1am, post-shower with wet hair and freshly moisturised all over. She was very pleased with herself. It had not been a bad night and now she was sparkling clean, contented and had the comfort of her king size bed all to herself. She slept like a log, but sadly only for five hours before having to get up for work. Why did she do this to herself and especially on a school night? It would make for a protracted week ahead, but she only had herself to blame!

It wasn't long before Lee messaged her on Monday morning. "I felt bad about last night. I thought you would have stayed. Was everything ok?" Lou went back with some message about it all being great. She had a good night with him, but just wanted to get home. That was all that really needed to be said about the night before, so she was a little shocked when he decided to tell her he had a confession and wanted to share it with her. 'Oh no. What's he going to tell me?' She thought to herself and wasn't entirely sure she wanted to find out. Experience told her that it was rare that anything good was going to come of this.

"Can I call you? Are you free?" There was a sense of urgency in his text. Lou confirmed she could talk and immediately her phone rang. "Hiya pet. Thank you. I just thought it would be easier to talk rather than type it all out. I hope you don't mind, but I just wanted to tell you something." Lou wasn't quite sure and was convinced that she probably would mind, but he was adamant about sharing. Lee went on to reveal what was troubling to the point of confession and confirmed, quite chirpily, that Lou's sixth sense was almost spot on the night before.

"You know you asked about the wardrobe door? Well when I usually film, it's on my Mac in the living room." What the fuck was he telling her? Lou was in shock and could feel the rage building up inside her. "What? Hold on. You *do* film your lovers? Do you normally ask their permission first?" She questioned him. Lee admitted that he didn't and that he'd recorded a few women he had invited back to his house. This proceeded to infuriate Lou above everything else. Not only was she angry with his actions but that he sounded all pleased with himself when he admitted, "You nearly had it there Lou. You were *so* close. I can't believe you almost guessed it." By the tone of his voice, Lee was clearly impressed, but this wasn't massaging Lou's ego in the slightest. She couldn't quite comprehend what she was hearing. "I'll show you," he went on to say. She was confused. He clearly already had something lined up for transmitting, as her phone pinged almost instantly and way before she had a chance to say "No thank you. You're all right. I don't need to see that." She was too late. Whatever it was had just arrived on her device.

Lou wanted nothing more than to end this conversation right now. Instead, from the frozen frame that appeared now on her phone, it was obvious that video footage of one of his liaisons was now in her possession. She was becoming more repulsed with Lee. How could he do something so low? He'd come across as a really nice guy: funny, caring and thoughtful. How had she misjudged him? Not only that, but now he was starting to make her skin crawl and that was before she absorbed what had arrived on her phone. "Sorry love: I've already sent it," he chirped. "Right," Lou said. "I'm going to go. I've got to get on with work." It was a lame excuse, but all she could think of to get out of this conversation. "I'll message you later," she finished with. He sounded down beat and said he'd speak with her then, but Lou wasn't so sure.

Lou's mind was racing. Only hours before, in the discomforts of his dog-stench of a bedroom, he'd been devouring her intimate parts with his tongue. (It was just as well he was so good at it too, otherwise she'd have cleared out of there earlier than she did!) Now she was feeling a little disgusted that she'd been quite so intimate with someone who was not only deceitful and calculated, but disrespectful too.

Now Lou found herself with a dilemma. On her phone was footage of Lee with an unsuspecting female, having unknowingly filmed sex. What's more, because of Lou's phone settings, it was now stored in her photos. From the still image, she could see a lady positioned straddled across Lee on the sofa. Should she play it to see what he had recorded? Was it fair on whoever the star was if she did view it? Lou decided she wouldn't intrude. Instead she deleted it and messaged Lee to tell him exactly how she felt.

There were no holds barred. She gave him her full verbal throttle and explained that she never wanted to see him again. "These women you've filmed: it's a violation of their privacy. You haven't asked for their consent and it's utterly unforgiveable that you've done that in the first place, let alone then sending it on to someone else." It was Lee's turn to be surprised. "It's ok pet. I wouldn't send it on to anyone else," he retorted. "But you already did!" She exclaimed! "No Lou, I only sent it to you 'cause I trust you." Total dismay followed for Lou. Was he really this stupid? How had she let him so close to her? "Well I deleted it. Please don't send me anything like that again. I don't want to see it and you could at least do her the honour too of telling her you filmed the pair of you. She deserves to know." Lee didn't seem too enamoured with this idea but agreed. He would tell her, but didn't mention any of the other women he had betrayed. It sounded like a lie to Lou, but she wasn't prepared to continue this 'friendship' to find out if he ever did.

Lou distanced herself from him from that point forward. She did hear from him a few weeks later, when he messaged to say he now understood where Lou was coming from. He'd apparently come clean and told the ladies what he'd done. Lou didn't believe him. He asked if she were ever likely to return to the party where they had met and if she would accompany him as his partner? Lou declined and never did go back to that venue. She didn't want to run into him again.

It had been a shocking reminder to Lou to trust her instincts and act on them. If she'd continued their activities with the wardrobe door open, who knows who could have been sent footage of her going full pelt on his penis? Despite having been on camera in her earlier days in this swinging lifestyle, Lou had learned that in order to maintain her privacy, it had to be respected. Lou was no prude. She'd had sex in public on numerous occasions and loved being the centre of attention, but it was on her terms. She was in control when she chose to put on a show. Even in sex clubs or parties, permission is always sought for any activities. The difference with Lee, however, was that he took the option of choice away, which wasn't his rite, nor was it right. Lou vowed never to see him again and fortunately their paths have not crossed since.

Chapter 4 - Hungry ladies

'It's always the quiet ones eh?' Lou thought to herself. The beautiful blond German lady called Tania appeared demure, even a little shy, in the company of the boisterous 'birthday gang' on the beach. They went to Gran Canaria, her favourite island, every November to celebrate the male contingent joint birthdays of the group. Lou was initiated as she shared the same birthday as one of them and was invited to join the collective and their guests who were enjoying cava on the glorious beach. The naked attire was so naturally accepted that she took little notice of their physiques, well not obviously any way.

Lou joined them for a bite to eat during a couple of hours of drinking, chatting and soaking up the sunshine. Somehow they managed to communicate with various levels of German and English being exchanged, along with made up sign language and a little Google Translate thrown into the mix when things got really tricky. This was exacerbated by the alcohol and came with some entertaining charade guesswork, particularly when purposely adding in innuendo in the different languages. The snacks from the kiosk soaked up some of the booze but proper food was required, and so they made their way to respective separate abodes before the night's events unfolded before them.

After their hotel restaurant visit, the German group

was heading out to a bar Lou was unfamiliar with, in a shopping centre she had not heard of either. Given how much Lou loved adventures, she accepted their invitation and agreed to meet them there later.

Lou was happy to wander down to a local restaurant near the Cita Centre on her own, once she had freshened up after the beach. She had intended on feasting on some papas arrugadas with mojo sauce. They had been on her mind all afternoon! The dish was considered a starter or side order, but Lou found the portion was just the right size and she enjoyed the salted potatoes, washed down with a couple of the local small beers: perfect!

Once Lou was suitably nourished, she hailed a taxi and made her way to the Nino Centre. To her surprise, it was looking a bit neglected and somewhere she wasn't entirely sure she felt safe being dropped off at. As it was now almost 11pm, most of the shops were shut and there was not a soul around. It was a little off-putting for this usually confident partygoer. But persevere she could and maintaining her head held high, she did not wish to appear vulnerable as strolled inside the centre. Lou soon found the club she was looking for, but it wasn't easy. There was a discreet door above which the name was adorned. She had missed it on the first glance across her surroundings. The thumping music beats coming from below ground were muted by the thick entrance doors, which once opened, let the bursting sounds spill out above, as Lou was welcomed inside.

Coming from the somewhat bright shop fronts above, it took Lou a while for her eyes to adjust to the darker setting, as she focused on the layout before her. It was just a few steps down first to the reception area, where payment would be taken. As a single lady she had to pay ten euros and that entitled her to a free drink too. From there on, were more steps to where the club was in full swing. Lou quickly perused the scene. To the right hand side were lockers and some single men at the bar. To the left, more couples were chatting, either at the bar or on the sofas. Others were already dancing and messing about on the two poles that were located on a small step up from the dance floor. There were a decent number of people already here considering it was relatively early still, however Lou's pals were yet to arrive.

The overwhelming stench of cigarettes was already filling the air. Lou had forgotten what it was like to have people openly smoking within an establishment. It was like London 30 years ago, before social smoking became a thing and before it then became an anti-social behaviour instead. Either way, in Spain you appreciated that when the locals came out to play, the air would be pretty foggy!

It wasn't long at all before Lou found the bar was far too smoky for her liking and it was starting to annoy her. She wondered when her preference on this topic had changed so dramatically? Being an ex-smoker herself from way back when, the odour really grated on her, not to mention the secondary damage being endured. She had been in an open-fronted bar with the Germans the year before and remembered how the smell lingered in her hair and on her clothes despite the natural ventilation. It reminded her of youth clubbing days (at Oscars and the Ilford Palais) where you could smoke openly in the venues and your shoes would stick to the disgustingly worn carpets. You'd wake up the next day stinking like an ashtray and immediately need fumigating!

Lou's German friends messaged to say they had been delayed but were now on route to join her. Could she line up some handsome men to entertain the girls when they arrived? Lou read the message discreetly before placing her bag and phone into one of the lockers and away for the evening. She decided to order her 'free' rather strong gin and tonic and took another sweeping glance at both sides of the bar before taking the tour that was offered as she paid to get in. It seemed that single men were allowed to one side and could only join the couples' side if invited across the bar! This could work. She would decide later which side of the bar was more profitable for her night's pleasure.

The tour showed Lou the full facilities and layout of the club. To the back of the bar were a series of rooms for differing requirements. There was the usual bondage area, for those who preferred more of that kink, a glory hole wall space, and three varying size rooms for private or public use: one of which was already occupied and sounded like a good pounding was taking place.

Following the overview, Lou returned to the bar to find her friends had arrived and were way more than a little bit tipsy. They had their usual hugs and within minutes, Tania was on the prowl and soon eating up men for breakfast! Lou was in awe of her tenacity. This was a woman after her own heart! She was on fire and it came as a bit of a shock to Lou because her husband was usually the more outgoing of the couple at the beach (earlier and every time Lou had met them). It was he who was usually boisterous, flirting and suggestive, while she had been in her own world, never saying a great deal – in the daylight that was! Now the roles had certainly been reversed as it became clear this was a cuckold relationship. He watched on as she danced with two different men and then took them both off to one of the playrooms. He stayed at the bar drinking and laughing with the others, who were enjoying the ambience first before deciding their own fate for the night. He wasn't fazed or upset, but instead was having a great time messing around.

When Tania returned from her first round of the night, there was not a hair out of place, just a knowing grin across her face as she signalled for Lou to meet one of her spent partners. Lou couldn't really hear or understand what she was saying until she motioned that his cock was enormous. 'OK, I understand that,' Lou implied. Tania was offering him to her, but Lou had other intentions. She had her eye on a cute Spaniard she'd spotted across the bar. He wasn't loud or animated, like her companions and many others on that side. Instead, he looked a little shy. He was slight, toned and appeared comfortable in his own skin. He was equally content to be sat there taking it all in: absorbing the ambience of the night. There was something she found quite inquisitive about him and Lou knew she wanted to get to know him better.

Lou made her way across to where he was perched and he gestured for her to join him. "Are you having a good night?" he asked in that lovely sultry accent, which she absolutely adored, and so the conversation started. Jorge was 34 and around 5' 8" with swept back, thick dark brown hair. His eyes were those sparkling green Spanish variety Lou worshipped and his English was very good. He worked in law enforcement on the island, although he looked a little embarrassed to admit that. This didn't scare Lou off, which he confessed he thought it might well have done. He came across as very polite and respectable, even whilst looking to pick up in a swingers' club. It reminded Lou of a conversation she had with her daughter many moons ago. It went something along the lines of "swingers are quite normal you know. It's not always about sex all the time and it's not always seedy." Lou felt it was important to explain that being part of this alternative lifestyle didn't mean you had to be sordid with it!

However, on this occasion in the scene, that's exactly what Lou did want to be! Shallow as it was, she instantly acknowledged he had a great body on him too: one that she wished to explore. It reminded her of Latex Man (*see Vanilla Extract*), and Lou couldn't help but think he was just as strong. Despite the initial coy demeanour and responses, Jorge was now starting to display a growing confidence, as his flirting took on a new form of its own, fuelled by Lou's brimming energy and need for sexual fulfillment. This new pair was bouncing off each other verbally and soon to be physically too.

Lou was quick to instigate the move away from the bar to the play areas behind. "Shall we just cut to the chase and go next door?" Well there was no point in beating around the bush. They both knew what they wanted and were about to get it. She hadn't seen anyone move quite as fast as Jorge abandoning his drink and stool and grabbing her hand to lead her away. Oh she liked his style. He was as much up for this as she and Lou just hoped she wouldn't be disappointed. There was the risk that he wouldn't live up to expectations or match the desire that had just been created in those few moments checking each other out. At times like this, Lou's adrenalin was pumping and she was ready to indulge.

On the way to the play area, she crossed paths with Tania once more. She was leading another incredibly well-hung man by his penis to one of the rooms and had a rather menacing look on her face. This was a side to her that Lou had never seen before. Tonight her desire was to get properly fucked and judging by the size of the equipment she was dragging with her, that's exactly what she was going to achieve! "You have him next Lou!" she wistfully shouted as she drove him into a room and slammed the door shut. Lou wasn't so sure about that! To be honest, Lou wasn't sure there would be much of either of them left!

Back to Jorge, who had looked on in amusement at Tania's antics. "She is a friend of yours?" he asked, looking a little bewildered. "Yes, she is. She seems to be on a mission tonight and a little more wild than I have ever seen her before!" He smiled sympathetically as they made their way to an open area, where the leather-covered bed was unoccupied and waiting for them. It was on full show for anyone passing through the play area, which didn't bother Lou. She was all on for putting on a performance. "This is ok?" he asked. She nodded in agreement as she climbed on top and began to remove her dress. "One moment," he insisted and lowered it down back onto her body. "I want to kiss you." With that, he slipped his smooth tongue inside Lou's mouth and so began their intimate discovery of each other.

She was right: he was strong. His right arm scooped her jaw as his left went behind the back of her head. Lou

48

was locked in his hold as their tongues became acquainted. 'Thank goodness for that,' Lou thought. It was rampant and exciting, and he was actually engaging, which was a very good sign. You could tell so much from a kiss. 'Oh he would be just fine when it came down to the sex itself,' Lou thought. Well you would certainly hope so, but it wasn't always the case. There was one particular Jaguar F-type owner she had dabbled with earlier that year. His banter was funny and he made her laugh whenever they met. He'd even rolled his extensive tongue out below his chin to demonstrate what he had on offer.

Sadly the let down was revealed when she decided to surprise him one day as he arrived at her home to take her for lunch. Lou decided to have the full 'secretary' look going on, with tight pencil skirt, open striped blouse revealing her uplifting bra, stockings, suspenders and heels on show for him as she opened the door. It had been a gamble as they had only kissed and flirted until this point. He had taken her to lunch on many occasions and she was at a loss to fathom out why he didn't pursue having sex with her, despite the banter. Today was going to be different: or at least she hoped so. Lou did have a moment of panic just before she answered the door and wondered if she had read the situation completely wrong. Maybe he just wanted to be friends who lunched rather than friends with benefits? It was too late now…

Fortunately he was suitably turned on when she exposed her outfit to him, closed the door and led him upstairs. There was no doubt that he was very much willing to be taken too. He had smiled, said, "Ooh, hello" and happily followed. In the bedroom they finally kissed and Lou was pleased that the never-ending tongue happily explored her tonsils and then her most delicate area. He certainly had the oral skills with that snake of a tongue and Lou had effortlessly covered it in her juices. Upon returning the delight, came the unavoidable disappointment, when she unzipped his trousers to disclose what he had packing inside. It was tiny. 'Oh no, what a shame,' she'd thought to herself. After all the teasing about how he would fulfill her over the past two months, now she was faced with this rather small appendage. Trying not to disclose the setback, Lou made the best of a bad situation. At least this meant deep throating would be easy! Her mascara would remain intact too! Funnily enough she never heard from him again, so maybe he had his own insecurities where that was concerned.

Lou was about to find out if Jorge was carrying a larger tool in his pants! Their intense kissing led to him moving his hands to around her back and drawing her into his broad, hairy, tanned chest. Here their torsos were held together and she could feel his growing erection rubbing against her. Lou couldn't help but grind into it, making circular motions with her hips. She was feeling really horny now and wanted nothing more than for him to take her dress off and lap up her juicy pussy.

Jorge was certainly building the tension. 'Damn', Lou was thinking. 'Come on. I so, so want this.' Sensing she was becoming impatient, he said, "Let me undress you." 'YES, YES, YES!' Lou was thinking but held it together, maintaining her cool exterior. "I would like that Jorge." Bloody hell she was good at this! Inside she was screaming 'GET ON WITH IT!'

Slowly Jorge lifted the hem of her dress over her shoulders and head, and then placed it to the side of her on the bed. Now he held her shoulders and stared directly in the eyes. "Let me look at you… You are beautiful." 'Yeah, yeah,' Lou was thinking: 'For fuck sake, let's just do this!' Her impatience was at an all-time high as her desire was reaching tipping point. This would be the last time she maintained her self-control. If they didn't get it on now, she would have to pounce on him instead!

"I want to lick every inch of you Lou. I want to taste every drop." 'Fucking do it' she instantly thought and wondered momentarily if she had actually shouted it out loud. She pulled away from him, kicked her shoes off to the side and laid down immediately. No more small talk or pleasantries. His look of surprise was ignored and her body language said all he needed to know: 'Let's get on with it!'

The delicate touch of his tongue on her neck was just the start. He was working his way down to her now pulsating vagina. She could almost hear the beat from higher up on the bed! Lou wondered if this was just a short tease and he would soon dive straight inside her wet lips or would he take his time and work his way down gradually? And why exactly was she so horny tonight? It may have been something to do with the hot sun beating down on her pelvis earlier in the day. She loved naked sunbathing and the heat on her 'flower' always turned her on at the beach. That was down to the sun's rays but also the liberation of wearing nothing but her own skin.

Jorge had taken the decision to spend a while on her breasts before heading lower. He reached underneath her back and undid her bra. Lou wriggled out of it to speed

51

things along. As he reached up on her body, she felt his erection caress her stomach and this left her wanting more. His gentle nibble of her left nipple sent tingles straight to her clitoris and she wondered if she was actually dripping onto the bed as he began to massage her right nipple in his fingers. Lou began to relax now. Why was she rushing this? 'Let's just lay back and enjoy every sensation.' Suddenly calm was restored as Lou breathed in deeply and enjoyed the attention. That was better. 'Relax Lou,' she told herself.

From the corner of her eye, Lou spied another man at the side of the bed, leaning casually against the wall, but clearly enjoying the spectacle before him. He had no shirt on and she could see he was definitely an avid gym-goer. She noticed that he was down to his pants too. Who knew where he had left his clothes? His quads were clearly defined, as were his biceps, triceps and pec's. What a fine figure he was and one potentially for later, or so she thought. He had seen her staring at him, as her tits were being flicked, sucked and kneaded. It was turning her on as he watched with intent. Lou wondered how Jorge would feel about him joining their soiree?

Lou grabbed Jorge's arm. He looked up and she indicated to him that someone else wanted to join in. She was testing the water here, as she had no idea what his reaction would be. "Whatever you want Lou. I'm happy if you are happy," he said. That was all she needed to carry on with this newly found interest. She gave the stranger the nod and he proceeded to join them.

Lou wasn't entirely sure where he would assist to start or where Jorge would prefer him, so she let the natural course of events take their own turn. Jorge wanted to engorge himself on her pussy and was pulling her knickers down at the sides. Lou raised her buttocks in the air, so he could easily remove them and he had full access to her body, as their new guest resumed action with her nipples. Well this really was a treat and just what Lou desired: one man dining on her moist cunt as another sucked her tits hard. Fuck this was exciting. She reached across to the new man, grabbed at his throbbing cock and removed it from his pants. Now she had a handful to fondle as Jorge worked her up into a rhythm. Her right hand reached down to the back of his head and she pushed him deeper into her. A constant leaking of cum was escaping her body and it felt incredible. She could keep this up all night if they could!

The new attendee to their private party was also wanting more and Lou happily obliged by pulling his penis closer to her mouth. He was ripe for the taking and ready for a good sucking. Jorge continued his feast as Lou now began her own. Her left hand was gliding up and down the new penis, and then with her tongue replacing her hand, she cupped his balls underneath him, as she tasted his member. This added to her excitement and so continued her juices running.

Lou noticed to her right that a rather disheveled Tania had emerged from the closed room. Her hair was all over the place and she looked like she had enjoyed a jolly good session with her enormous conquest.

She smiled over in appreciation and yelled, "Lou Lou, you greedy girl. Here's another one for you!" She forcefully pushed her man towards Lou. Unfortunately he wasn't quite ready for another round just yet, but he was eager to replace Jorge at her pussy, to which neither

53

of them nor Lou had any objections.

Jorge stood to her right and now it was his turn to receive her oral pleasure, as Lou focused her attention on him and returned to wanking the man to her left. This was just getting better and better as far as Lou was concerned! She had a cock in her mouth, another in her hand and someone happily munching on her vagina. "You're welcome!" Tania bellowed and laughed as she made her way back to her German friends.

And that was how it came to be that Lou had three men at her disposal. It wasn't her first MMMF (male, male, male, female combination) but the first with all of them of non-English origin. In fact she wasn't even sure if they could all speak English, not that it mattered right now. They could all speak the language of sex, and very well she had discovered first-hand!

Lou thought it only right that Jorge should be the first to fuck her. It had all begun with him this evening and so in her mind, it was his right. She removed his swollen genitalia from her mouth and with her eyes focused on his, she said, "I want you inside me Jorge." She had wanted him all night, but been distracted by the other additions to their naughty gathering. "I have been waiting to hear you say that," he responded and made his way down to exactly where she wanted him, pushing the thirsty man aside. Looking a little put out, he wasn't sure where he should be, so took up the position Jorge had just left behind.

Before he slowly entered Lou, she double-checked he had a condom. Of course he did. She had no need to ask him. He slipped it out from his clothes and quickly put it on as she watched. Lou ceased touching the other men as he slid inside. She wanted to savour this first sensitive moment, which they both shared alone, despite the others at the sidelines. Their eyes were locked in and then the action really started!

Lou wasn't sure if Jorge had to prove himself to her or in front of the other men, but he was determined to pound her hard. His thrusts sent her to the back of the bed, to the point where she had to say to stop momentarily as she was hitting her head on the wall! Jorge dragged her back down the bed by her hips and resumed his rampage. Lou struggled to maintain the even blowjobs she was attempting to administer to the sides of her, wanting neither man to have more attention than the other. She was fair like that: even while her body was being throttled – in the loveliest kind of way!

Lou was able to give Jorge the occasional look between her legs as her pumelled her hard, checking he was ok. He was having just as good a time as she was, but she sensed, quite understandably, that he was growing tired. She suddenly had a pang of concern for him. Something in that moment made her want it just to be the two of them now. Lou was no longer interested in having 'conveyor belt sex' as she termed it. A younger Lou would have been thrilled to have had three different men fuck her right there one by one, but then in the heat of the moment, she wanted to end the foursome and just be with him. And when Lou had a feeling in her gut, she tended to act on it. So that's exactly what she did.

"I'm sorry guys, but that's all folks!" Lou cared not that she sounded like the end of a cartoon animation! This merriment was about to be terminated and she was just fine about that. After initial looks of disappointment, the additional men accepted their fate, pulled away and gathered their clothing. There were no hard feelings, as there never tended to be, as everyone had enjoyed their interactions and were now smiling. Jorge looked a little puzzled. "Did I not satisfy you Lou?" She pulled him towards her and told him that she wanted him all to herself. A huge smile appeared on that beautifully tanned face. "Then I must take you home," he beamed and she agreed, but first they would drink and dance, which they did with her other friends, before he drove her home and they continued their lustful coupling.

Lou's gut feel was right about him too. He really was a gent, as she sensed he would be. In the morning after some more naughtiness, he drove her to the airport, and off she travelled back to the UK, with more delicious memories of her favourite fun-filled island.

Chapter 5 - Sunny Sunday afternoon

Lou had always been partial to a fit man and this particular ex-professional rugby player had become a very good friend over the years, as well as an exceptional lover. Their interactions were always different, incredibly hot, randomly funny and inevitably both of them would be in fits of laughter at the most inappropriate of times: usually when naked and interlocked!

On this particular Sunday, with no kids around, Lou had already been to the gym, cut the grass, hung out the washing and was now drying herself after a bath. With her towel wrapped around her bottom half, she sat on her bed and decided to catch up with her socials. A guy from work was flirting on Whatsapp and was asking for naughty pictures, which of course she declined. At this relatively new employer, she had taken the stance of not mixing business with pleasure. Whilst she'd had her fill of such liaisons at her last place of work, she was keeping it professional here. That is, unless she was really interested and to be honest, if anything was going to go on with Lou and him, then it would have happened by now. (Funny how women can accept such things. Men take a little bit longer for that to sink in, if it ever does. They can try and try ad infinitum, sometimes never getting the message!)

And there he was. Robert had just returned from a conference in San Francisco and was now on Dad-duties at home despite the jetlag just setting in. They had spoken on Whatsapp earlier in the day (as was the norm) and they joked about him paying her a booty call later that evening. It was unlikely, to be fair, but given they had similar sexual appetites, it was something they both yearned for to happen. It had been at least one month since he was last deep inside her and the longing was far from dissipated.

Noticing he was online as she relaxed, Lou reached out with, "What time should I expect you?" It was asked in jest and the humorous banter continued. "How late can I arrive?" Partially hopeful and partially playful, she teased, "Well any time before 9am tomorrow works for me. How about you?" A series of emojis followed. The seed had been planted and was now growing. There was a strong desire to have each other again because their sex was utterly mind-blowing every single time. It was the kind of intercourse that was so intense, he even had to remind her to breathe when they were fully absorbed in the moment and locked into each other. The gaps in between their mammoth sessions just made them grow hungrier for each other. What a shame the responsibilities of life had such a tendency to get in the way!

As Lou was lying on the bed, with her towel now draped across her body, it was falling open at the centre. Her hand swept across her stomach and found itself at her most intimate part. She brought her feet together and let her knees fall open as the towel held on to her sides. It was just enough of a gap to see her newly shaven Brazilian pussy poking through. What a beautiful picture that would make: even more so with her right hand reaching inside to her precious gift. It was artistic, teasing and erotic. Robert would love it! Immediately a photo was taken and soon on its way across the ethers. He was someone Lou trusted implicitly to send such intimate images to. Lou was right about him liking it, when she received, "That's so hot baby!"

"I'm touching myself Robert and it feels tingly. Can you please come here later, so you can help?" Again the cheekiness continued but this time he asked, "Show me how wet you are." Lou was a little surprised. It wasn't something he'd ever asked of her before. Did he mean a picture of her wet pussy? Did he want a video call? Was he looking for a recording of her playing with herself? Lou decided instead to take a picture of her right hand. Carefully she lined up her phone so she could snap the photo at the optimum moment. Having lifted her forefinger from her vagina, there was a stream of sticky clear fluid joining them both and that's what she sent across to him. It reminded her of morning dew on a spider's web on an autumn morning, which was equally beautiful! She didn't mind that her labia were on show as he'd seen them many, many times before. What mattered was that he could see exactly how moist she had made herself.

It had been two days since Lou had last had a climax. Lying on her bed and stroking her fingers across her clit, Lou could feel it wouldn't be long before she achieved her next one. Whilst she felt she needed this release, she didn't want it too soon and even though she would be able to come and come again, Lou was enjoying being this close to peaking, but saving herself for a little bit longer. When Lou did allow the orgasm to arrive, it would be super-intense, however for now she would continue the 'edging' and keep herself on the brink of explosion.

The saliva Lou had used when she first began to touch

herself needed no further refill. Her body had started to create its own lubrication, which she was now smothering across her bean. Sliding either side of it, she moved her fingers inside her. Whilst that did feel good, it would have been even better if someone else were doing it for her. She passed her dampened fingers across her right breast and ensured her nipple was now wet too. The breeze from her open bedroom window soon made it erect and ready for some tweaking. Lou did the same for the left nipple and then imagined two other people playing with her breasts while she masturbated. Damn she was horny!

It appeared that Lou was turning Robert on too. He'd already told her before that he had the kids this afternoon, and his wife's friend's kids too, as the ladies were out training for a triathlon. Being 'daddy daycare' Lou hadn't expected to be speaking with him this afternoon, let alone getting this fruity with one another. Yet here they both were and each with an itch that needed scratching. As they were so comfortable in each other's presence, whether in person or via video call, it came as no surprise when he suggested, "Come to the bathroom with me, but we'll have to be quiet." She was happy to oblige. 'Ooh how naughty,' Lou thought.

Robert soon set his phone up on the side in the shower and it was pointing directly at him as he turned on the water ever so slightly. The sound would be a signal to the children that he was busy and to be left alone. It was the perfect cover, yet quiet enough to alert him of any problems outside of the bathroom.

Robert's natural colouring had always complimented Lou's whenever they were one. The contrast of skin tones was beautiful: coffee and cream. And his cock! Well his penis she referred to as 'Monster Cock' due to its length and strength! It always surprised her how he kept that package all contained in his pants, when his figure was slight, albeit toned and without an ounce of body fat. It fell out of his underwear and just kept going! And whilst she could barely deep throat three quarters of it, Lou somehow managed to ride it in its entirety when she was on top. Lou had never quite fathomed out how her body achieved that. It was magic! However it worked, it did perfectly and it was an incredible feeling of him being as high as he could possibly go inside without causing damage! (Although they did have to change positions a number of times during the course of their many encounters, when it had become uncomfortable.)

Right now there was no chance of discomfort from afar, instead just a little mischievous Sunday afternoon fun, made all the more exciting by being spontaneous. It was undoubtedly Lou's fault, as she was all horny and needed some attention. Robert was only too pleased to get involved, taking out some of his own pent up frustrations in the easiest possible manner: shower sex. It would even be easy to dispose of the evidence, once the given mission was accomplished! How brilliant too that iPhones are waterproof! Robert took sheer delight in showing Lou how stimulated she had made him. His ample weapon took very little additional encouragement before he let it off as she watched. Lou briefly saw the thick produce erupt before it was washed away.

Lou was pleased Robert had relieved himself, more so because it was unexpected, but it brought her no other self-satisfaction. She was still wanting to have her own orgasm, but now wasn't really a convenient time. Her

61

children could walk in at any time, as her bedroom door was always open and it would look a little odd if it were now closed.

Robert smugly dried himself off and then returned to his Dad-duties. Lou would save her own self-indulgence for later, when her own little darlings were asleep and she could relax whilst relieving herself ever so sweetly.

Chapter 6 - A blessing of unicorns

Lou was told that the collective noun for a group of unicorns is a 'blessing' and that's certainly what one unsuspecting young man received when he went to work that cold December night in Liverpool...

Lou had met her original Unicorn friend at a Halloween event in London. As you'd expect, it wasn't just fancy dress, but a full on swingers' party, and she was introduced to Anna, who was there with her ex-military boyfriend. Lou was there with some of her Flavas ladies and had taken Snake Hips along to share with the group, much to his delight!

Lou's group had originally been due to host their own party, but when the owners of the hired apartment found out what sort of shenanigans were planned, they hastily cancelled the booking. Rebecca found them an alternative gathering and this is what led to them all sharing a naughty night together. She particularly remembered Snake Hips pounding her friend Lucy, and Lou being the subject of a joint rope tying and gushing demo lesson! That was following Lucy making her gush for a laugh very early on in the evening and then Lou returning the gesture a moment later! Lou also remembered how she enjoyed massaging Anna's breasts while she was having sex, but alas Snake Hips was not allowed to join them!

That was two years before Lou found herself heading towards Liverpool straight from work late on a chilly

Friday afternoon. She wasn't sure how many ladies would be joining her at the hotel suite that was booked, but she was assured it would be a great evening. The Unicorns' usual arrangement would be to share a themed Friday night all together and then have their partners (boyfriends, fuck-buddies or husbands) join them on the Saturday night, where they would all party as a group at a swinging club.

Upon arriving at the station, Lou messaged 'Nana' to let her know she was now walking the short walk to the hotel. Nana was Anna's best friend and Lou met her the summer before at a club in St Neots. The ladies immediately hit it off, with very similar personalities and senses of humour, as well as their no bull shit attitudes. Nana had also arranged for Lou to have one of the suite beds to sleep in, given she had travelled so far to join them. How very thoughtful!

At the reception desk, Lou took a while to take in the décor. It was artistically painted, with a nautical theme and impressively grand. Nana soon came down to welcome Lou and help her with any bags. The girls shared a massive hug and immediately started nattering away like old pals. Lou had packed a small trolley dolly as she had outfits for both saucy nights as well as the daytime shopping planned for the next daytime. A bottle of gin was also onboard, but tonic was already taken care of, she had been informed. Lou easily took it up to the beautiful Titanic Suite, which would be her home for the next two nights.

Inside the room Anna jumped up to greet her. Interestingly she was dressed in a pink onesie, which Lou quickly came to see was in the design of their favourite mythical creature. It had been a while and Anna was keen to make Lou feel welcome. A bottle of prosecco was already in motion and a glass soon poured for their travelled, now honorary Unicorn enlistee.

Lou was able to unpack quickly as the reminiscing continued and before the next guests arrived. In total, seven other women joined the party, and all being girls together, it was very easy to fall into the comfortable chatting about just about anything and everything. Some were prepared for tonight, others had to shave, items of clothing were being brought to lend to others, accessories were being swapped, etc. etc. Lou felt this was an easy group to get on with and be a part of.

It wasn't long before Lou found herself in the massive bathtub with a newly found acquaintance called Lonnie. She was particularly friendly and really went out of her way to include Lou in any conversations, particularly filling in gaps where it was obvious Lou wouldn't have been able to follow. The group had enjoyed many outings prior to this weekend and recalled some hilarious encounters.

Lou was in the tub first, freshening up after her long train journey and Lonnie asked if she minded her jumping in. More getting to know you ensued while both ladies proceeded to shave their armpits, legs and bikini areas! They shared details of their partners, kids, jobs and preferences. Lou was finding it incredibly easy to feel at ease with the Unicorns!

Once freshened up, it was time for everyone to get into their clothes for the evening, which tonight was all about Moulin Rouge. Ladies were asked to wear something appropriate in red and they were all acutely

65

happy to be making the effort to fulfil their burlesque desires. Lou had packed a red corset with black trim, fishnet stockings and usual killer heels. She brought some dangling black earrings, which she totally forgot to wear in all the excitement of all getting made up together.

Nana and others had brought food to the gathering. The kitchen area was packed full of different delights and there was no way anyone would be going hungry tonight. They wouldn't go thirsty either, as the bottles of gin, vodka, prosecco, wine and lots of tonic, were overflowing on the worktop. 'These girls sure know how to party!' Lou thought to herself. She would have to pace herself with the alcohol or else she'd be wasted in no time!

Women do love to chat and they like a good selfie too. Lou lost count of the number of pictures being taken within the group, to the point that she put her own phone away and said she would download any from their shared Whatsapp group. Earlier in the evening, photos were mainly of the sexy outfits and poses of play, even if they were just in jest. As the stiff drinks were consumed, any lingering inhibitions, of which there were not many Lou could identify, evaporated in the shared all-feminine soiree before them.

As with all such gatherings, the date didn't work for some of the group. One lady who was unable to attend had arranged for a 'bare-bum butler' to arrive at 9pm, by which time, their spirits were elevated, just as were their voices. Screams of gratitude and delight sounded out as the poor boy was welcomed into the den! He was a mere 17 and didn't quite know what he was walking into. The ladies swarmed on him like curious bees, but Lou felt a little bit sorry for him. He was clearly gob-smacked, but relaxed a little when he realised they were harmless predators, although some were keen to see if he was bare-bottomed when he walked in. To their delight, the small apron covering his private parts revealed that his bum was almost naked, apart from the g-string pants that were holding his dignity in one place!

When the initial shock of his welcome settled down, Ben proceeded to do what he was being paid for, once Nana had given him a nudge. He'd been a little taken aback before he was called into action and his first drinks order was placed. Ben quickly dropped his bag in the corner of the kitchen and began to administer the thirsty ladies' drinks. They were going down even quicker and easier than before he had arrived and a new game of placing a shot glass in between some of the girls' derrieres seemed to delight them and Ben too. Lou wasn't so impressed with this and left them to it. She couldn't help but feel uneasy. Ben was younger than two of her children, for goodness sake.

Ben was permitted to have a few drinks himself, as long as no one told his boss, which obviously wouldn't happen. He was keen then to have photos taken with the Unicorn Blessing and share them with his pals. "You won't believe this job I'm on lads!" A series of pictures were taken and many of the group unashamedly flashed their breasts, but not Lou. Who knew where this would end up? She made her excuses and headed for the loo. It was enough time bought that when she returned, the shock factor had worn off and the girls had dispersed. Ben was also nowhere to be seen. It transpired that two of the group were giving him his own souvenir of the evening: a double blowjob, which was undoubtedly the first he would ever have experienced.

Lou didn't see him again, but imagined he would have departed the suite with a huge smile across his face. He'd probably have more pictures to prove it too, but that wasn't her concern. She did wonder where Nana was and soon found that she was passed out in one of the beds. Somehow before doing so, she had changed into her unicorn onesie too. (Lou wondered if all the ladies had matching loungewear!) Three other ladies had decided to go to a local pub, two had gone home due to childcare arrangements and the rest were in various states of undress in the suite. A few more mythical creature outfits were being brought out of bags and Lou's suspicions were confirmed.

Lou never slept in anything and tended to forget this when she went to nights away with her girlie friends. She found sleeping in anything was restrictive and had gotten used to being naked from her teenage years. Lonnie asked Lou if she had a onesie or pyjamas, to which she told of her sleeping preferences. "Well if you're laying down, you could always rest your pussy on my face." There was an instant twinge in Lou's precious place. 'That sounds like a rather delicious offer,' she thought to herself and one she most definitely was not going to turn down. "But I hardly know you," Lou mused and laughed before moving herself closer to Lonnie on the kingsize bed. "Allow me to introduce myself," she stated as she placed her hands either sides of Lou's tiny knickers and pulled them down to reveal her sensitive mound. Lou hadn't expected this, which made it all the more exciting.

Anna had been watching from the other side of the room. "I think you need a little more attention young

68

Lou," she said as she came over to join them. She undid the corset ties and pulled the outfit wider to expose Lou's breasts. It was Anna's moment to repay the fondling from two years before. Now Lou was in a state of ecstasy. She had two beautiful, vibrant and sexy women devouring her body and it was sending currents up and down her like wildfire. The piercing in Lonnie's tongue was making it increasingly difficult for Lou to control the rapidly building orgasm that she was fighting hard to keep at bay. Anna's delicate caress and soft nibbling of her nipples was already sending sparks to her clitoris that were being met by Lonnie's skilful mouth. Lou's back was arching and settling, arching and settling before she could hold it no longer. She had no time for words, to let them know it was coming, but they could read her body language. Boom: there it was in all its blessing of bisexual bliss, catapulting out of her shaking body. It was glorious and so utterly explosive that it took Lou a while to compose herself once more. Lonnie and Anna looked smug and obviously pleased with their joint mission, which had resulted in a complete success!

"Well I'm very pleased to meet you!" Lou spurted out between giggles, once she was able to! It had been quite an introduction and one she would not forget. And this was just the first night of the weekend!

Lonnie was tired and was looking for nothing more than to have given the gift to Lou, despite being offered. She had covered a night shift on the Thursday and was paying for it now. Anna was also keen to return to drinking some more and when the pub visitors returned, they continued to have more alcohol in the kitchen together. Not for Lou though. She was keen to retire as she also had a long day. To get some sleep now would be advantageous, given they would be clubbing the following night too.

Lou brushed her teeth, cleaned her girlie bits and then climbed in bed next to Nana, who was sleeping soundlessly. Her introduction to the Unicorns was completed and what an initiation it had been!

Chapter 7 - French fancy

Lou's journey to work changed when she decided to part with her employer of many years. No longer was she commuting to Canary Wharf but now to the City (in London) and she was enjoying the change in responsibilities as well as travel.

Lou wasn't quite sure what it was about Tubes and trains, but she seemed to have a number of encounters when using these modes of transport. Liverpool Street railway station would prove to be the scene of her next such meeting. Again it was purely by chance, with no online preamble or setting up. Back to the good old-fashioned way of meeting people: in person.

Lou was waiting outside the station for her friend Janice. It was 5.15pm on a dry Monday and the sun was shining. This summer had truly been the hottest that she could remember and she loved that going to work required no jacket or cardigan. Lou was less pleased that the trains became so stuffy, but nothing quite like London's underground system, which is where you'd be guaranteed to emerge a sweaty mess post-Tube travel.

Lou was a little early and she had actually forgotten that her friend was never usually on time. It had been a number of years since she'd seen her ex-work colleague and this evening promised to be a night of catching up and good old girlie chat. It was not supposed a time for charming men and indulging in that particular delight, but

Lou found (some might say 'created') exactly that exciting scenario.

Happily chatting away to her daughter on her mobile phone, Lou casually stood close to the McDonald's site just outside the station. Though she'd never been inside, it was a known landmark where the two women would meet. As always, it was busy area with people filling up just before departing from or arriving to the station. Now was no different, with the hustle and bustle of workers and visitors alike.

Lou paid little notice to those around her, other than the general surveying of the area she naturally undertook. That was until a rather gorgeous man walked past her, also talking on his telephone. It was his right arm raised up to his ear that first drew her attention. His crisp white shirt was tight against the bulging muscles beneath and when she continued to look him over, she then became transfixed on his face. He was staring at her too, which made her smile instantly. He had caught her in the act and his immediate response was to smile back, revealing a beautiful bright grin against his brown skin and equally dazzling eyes. 'Wow,' Lou thought. 'He's hot' and then he was gone.

Lou laughed to herself. It was one of those gratifying moments where she knew they were both now buzzing with appreciation; the flirtatious giving and receiving. You just couldn't beat it! She was now perked up with the shared moment, where she gave instant pleasure to someone else, just as he had done for her. Lou also knew he'd be feeling exactly the same, with a similar spark in his step. If only more people did that: there'd be so many more smiling people around town!

Moving into the station slightly, Lou looked out onto the open mezzanine area near the top of the escalators to see if Janice was heading her way. There was no sign of her. Lou planted herself there for a while and waited, whilst continuing her telephone catch up. It was good to be speaking with her second-born on her journey home. As Lou looked up and across the way, there he was again! His own conversation was still mid-flow too by the looks of it. Their eyes met once more and they both smiled. Was this a surprise for him too, Lou considered, or had he set it up? She had no idea. Lou also wondered if it was his wife or girlfriend that was keeping him occupied for so long?

For some reason, it appeared that every smoker in the vicinity now wanted to stand near Lou. It was time to relocate once more; back out to the courtyard and the cleaner air. Her conversation was coming to an end as her daughter had arrived home and Lou put her phone in her bag and zipped it closed. As she looked up, he was now standing in front of her and she couldn't be any happier. What a delightful surprise!

"I am sorry to trouble you, but I couldn't let this moment pass. If I did not stop and speak with you, I may never have seen you again. You are very beautiful and I would like to ask if you want to come for a drink with me now?" Lou was flattered and quite taken aback. How refreshing for a man (and a very cute man at that) to be so forthcoming and to add to the mystique, he had an adorable French accent! Lou explained that she was meeting her friend Janice for dinner shortly. Lou could see he was disappointed. "I'm free on Wednesday though, if you are too?" Instant redemption from the once sad face appeared before her. There was that smile again. Damn he was hot!

Amos explained that he was from Paris and had been talking with his parents prior to meeting Lou. In fact, he had cut the conversation short for fear of missing his opportunity to speak with her! How adorable! It wasn't long before his number was in her contacts and vice versa. How very exciting tonight had proven already (for them both)! Despite having just met, when they parted they shared a hug and promised that this chance meeting would continue in two days' time. "I very much look forward to Wednesday Lou." She felt exactly the same way!

Lou took great delight in sharing the story with Janice, who received it with a look of awe on her face. "How does this always happen to you?" Lou explained that it is mostly about maintaining eye contact. So many people walk around with their heads down, but when you look up and see other people doing the same, then miracles happen!

Amos messaged when the ladies were dining and told her how pleased he was that they had met. Lou reciprocated and said how she thought it was no coincidence. He felt the same way. He didn't believe in coincidences, which was entirely in line with Lou's thinking. It was all for a reason and she was excited to start this new adventure with this rather delectable man, wherever it led.

Being a little impulsive and rather impatient too, Lou suggested they meet for lunch the following day instead of waiting until Wednesday. It seemed Amos was equally keen and arranged to eat at a French restaurant in between both their work locations. Lou wasn't sure if it was the setting or their mood, but the lunch was not quite what she expected. She thought the conversation would be flowing and they would happily spend the time learning all about each other, which they did start. However, for some reason both of them felt a little awkward around each other this time and Lou wondered whether they had spoilt the fantasy-like unknowing excitement of the night before. Would it have been better to leave it to be exactly that; a glorious smile and knowing exchange of glances, and that was all?

More hugs were exchanged as they departed. Lou thanked Amos for lunch and they made their way back to their respective offices. 'Well that was disappointing' she thought, but she was undeterred. Their drinks plan for the following night was still on the cards, so she would see how that went before she wrote him off completely.

Lou was now three weeks into her new job and whilst she was starting to get a feel for how this different employer operated, she was finding that using her brain again to this extent was actually quite exhausting. It was a lot to absorb: new processes, new ways of working and unknown people. The new commute was also a challenge, with getting the train rather than jumping in her car and being home and dry within the hour. So when Amos mentioned drinks and dinner at a rooftop bar on the Wednesday, and given how their lunch had gone, Lou asked if he minded if they just went for a quick drink instead near the station before she departed for home. It was a safe card she wanted to play, just in case it didn't go as well as she hoped.

(Amos had only joined his company two months

before, so could sympathise with her tiredness.)

The pair chose to meet where their paths had first crossed a few nights before. As she rocked up, he was waiting, looking rather cool in his blue shirt and shades. They kissed cheeks and then he led her off to the Broadgate area, where there was an abundance of places to grab a chilled glass of wine. Tonight they were both relaxed and the conversation wasn't strained in the slightest. They sat on the sun-kissed granite and chatted about their days. Lou kicked off her peep-toe stilettos and sat cross-legged opposite him. (Her flowing flowery dress draped across her legs and maintained her decorum.)

As they were enjoying the evening and each other so much more, they decided to have another glass before Lou suggested they should have dinner after all. It was going way better than she thought and despite her fatigue, she was having a brilliant time learning all about this lovely man. She was incredibly surprised to learn he had membership to one of the swinging clubs she frequented. How funny! She hadn't expected that! He had only ever been there once and it wasn't a great experience by the sounds of it. Lou toyed with telling him how she could remedy that for him, but she didn't want to be too forward or too revealing of her social practices just yet.

Whilst sitting eating al fresco outside an Italian restaurant, Amos asked Lou what she was up to at the weekend. "Well, interestingly, it is a weekend where I don't have my children and for some strange reason I have no plans," she told him. This was unusual for Lou who normally filled her childfree weekends with other activities, whether it was clubbing, partying or visiting friends and family usually in other parts of the UK somewhere. This weekend there were no concrete plans. She'd said 'maybe' to a couple of events but nothing was definite just yet. It was always good to keep her options open and she could decide nearer the time.

"Would you consider coming away with me?" Amos put it out there and was not expecting the answer to be so quick and so definite. "Sure!" Lou burst out. He was shocked. "Really?" he questioned in disbelief and immediately he received the same response. "Yes, sure. Why not?" Lou's mind was made up. She'd spent enough time with him to judge his character and she could tell he was a good soul. "OK, so how would you feel about getting on a plane with me and going abroad for the weekend?" Again, Lou delivered the same reply. "As long as it's from Stansted," she said, as it was her local airport. "Tell me in the morning. You've had some wine. Maybe you would like to think about it overnight?" Amos reiterated, in case she needed an excuse to change her mind. There was no need. Lou's decision was made and it was final, much to Amos's surprise and delight.

Sitting across and staring at his eyes whilst the conversation and the alcohol flowed, Lou was hoping that he would invite her back to his flat near Battersea. There was no doubt they both felt incredibly attracted to each other and Lou was becoming very horny around him. Their flirting was delving into touching, albeit very respectful and controlled. Their hands were interlocked across the table and this was the first real shared touching they'd experienced other than greeting or departing hugs and kisses.

Lou could feel he was enjoying her caress too and so, after some consideration, she decided to speak a little more openly. "Part of me wants to jump in a cab and go back to yours where we can fuck each other silly, but another part wants to wait until our weekend away together." This was met with sparkling appreciation. "I feel the same too Lou. I am so hard for you right now and I'm not sure either." Lou felt an instant twinge in her pussy. Damn - what to do? What a dilemma; if they went back to his and the sex was mediocre, she wouldn't particularly then want to spend an entire weekend with him. But if the sex was good and they'd missed out on having it tonight, then that would be a complete waste. Amos laughed when she explained this to him, but totally understood where Lou was coming from. It made sense to him too. It was a risk they would have to take either way. Amid smiles and naughty thoughts, they decided to wait. As fantastic as it may be, it would make the adventure all the more memorable if they contained their passion just a little bit longer.

This sexual twosome made their way back to the station arm in arm and he waited for her train to come in. It would be another 15 minutes till it left and during this time they held each other close and had their first kiss. It was perfect. There was no slobbery saliva drooling down her face, but instead she discovered his chewable lips and dancing tongue. As she suspected, there was no fat on his body either, as he drew her into him. She could feel him against her and he was lean and firm. 'Mmmmm, let's hope the sex is worth the wait,' Lou thought to herself. It would be two sleeps until she found out, which seemed like forever!

They messaged on the journey home. Amos asked again whether she was sure she wanted to go away with him? Lou had no doubts at all. After giving some of her passport details for the flight, she suddenly had a minor panic. He could be stealing her identity, which of course he wasn't, but she only divulged part of the information just in case. "Please don't tell me where we are going," she implored of him. For years she had wanted someone to surprise her in this way. Lou had orchestrated similar holiday mysteries for her ex-husband and daughters in the past and she had always wanted someone to do this for her too. Now it was her chance. Amos agreed and admitted he would even keep the boarding pass to himself and let her swipe his phone through when they departed the airport. Lou was super charged now - how very exciting!

"It's funny how your children become your parents from time to time," Lou reflected when telling her good friend Millie about her experience with Amos so far. Lou's eldest child questioned whom he was, how long she'd known him and various other details for clarification. Lou was pleased to know she cared about her mother's security, but her daughter also knew she was a very good judge of character, who also relished adventures. She also had her tracked, using her phone's 'Find a Friend' app, so she could always pinpoint where she could be found. It was a mutual arrangement for peace of mind. Lou had enjoyed knowing where her daughter was too when she went off travelling around Asia.

Millie also wanted to make sure Lou wouldn't be murdered while she was off gallivanting with a complete stranger. Lou promised to check in wherever she landed and that's exactly what she did. Her only clue had been from Amos telling her to pack a bikini and a smile - perfect!

Standing at Stansted departures on Friday at 5pm, Lou was again on her mobile to her eldest. "What if this is an elaborate wind up and I'm plotted up here like a lemon?" Lou reflected and her daughter laughed. "Well at least you're not far from home if it is." That much was true. Lou mentioned that Amos had told her what time their flight was and that despite standing directly below the departure board, she had resisted the temptation to look up and see what destinations were showing at that given time.

As they continued speaking, Lou looked up to see Amos confidently approaching her. "Turns out it is real! He's walking towards me now." Lou told her daughter he had arrived, so she would be signing off. She would message when she landed, wherever that was, and she bid her goodbye for now. They said they loved each other, as was the norm with Lou and all of her children, and she now focused her attention on her rather delicious travel companion.

Amos was looking radiant and he was clearly as excited to see her, as she was to see him. Maybe he had thought she wouldn't show up too and that's why he was looking so relieved! Big hugs were exchanged like long-lost lovers before they made their way through the barriers. Lou was familiar with the airport as she frequented it frequently. She directed the way but was keen not to inadvertently discover their destination. As promised, he swiped her boarding pass and let her through so she wouldn't see. Their mystery tour was about to begin!

No one would ever have suspected these two hardly

knew each other. They surprised themselves that they were actually doing this! In the lounge she bought their drinks that they then preceded to consume a little too quickly. 'Why does time speed up before boarding a plane?' Lou wondered. It always seemed the same. There was always a slight panic to get to the gate for whatever reason, despite allowing plenty of leeway just in case. It probably boiled down to once rushing through this same airport to the gate for a flight to Marrakech. She had been leisurely enjoying the lounge and completely lost track of time. A mad dash to the gate finished with Lou and her then travel buddy being turned away as the gate closed. They were four minutes late and were not allowed to board. It had been incredibly frustrating, but today was fine. Whilst there was no rush, they did end up walking briskly to the gate just in case, and that's where Lou found out exactly where they were heading: Alicante for the weekend. "Ooh lovely. I've never been there!" She joyfully told Amos as they waiting to board.

On the plane they sat constantly touching. At times it was arm in arm, leg over legs, or similar. They were certainly carrying off this loved-up couple persona. They even believed it themselves; so convincing was this being into each other and so enjoyable too. Neither of them felt it was pretend or forced. It felt incredibly natural and no one would have suspected they had only actually met literally days before.

Lou was soon wrapped up with Amos. She could tell he was an adorable person and his heart was demonstrably pure. This was someone who gave up their time every Sunday morning to volunteer in a prison: giving hope to some of the offenders there. He'd also helped out in various other crises. What a star he was. Lou couldn't help but admire him, made easier by that cute face - obviously. His cut, firm body also helped, but only when the shallow, selfish thoughts took over her mind and she imagined the pair of them naked together. It wouldn't be long and Lou hoped this gamble was going to pay off!

At Alicante airport they went straight through arrivals to take a taxi. Neither of them had luggage, just carry-on, so that saved time. Half an hour after landing they were presented to the hotel and it looked impressive: clean, open and glamorous. They grabbed the lift to their room where they literally dropped their bags before moving straight to the rooftop bar. (Finally they had made their way to their first joint rooftop bar. She had put him off this previously the same week, which felt like a very long time ago now).

Lou had deliberated about what to travel in on this mysterious journey. Now that they were straight out following their arrival, she was pleased she had chosen a flowing, clinging red cotton dress. It was full length and casually gripped her in all the right places. It was very flattering of her curvy figure and she felt sexy in it too: a winner in her book (and his, it transpired).

Amos chose rum and Coke, while Lou went for a gin and tonic. Being in Spain, the alcohol measures were massive and they were both rocking by the time they finished their drinks. Lou wondered if Amos was a little self-conscious, as he chose to decline a refill, whereas she opted for another one. Maybe he was considering the performance he would be soon putting in, which was a first for them both together, given they decided to wait for any physical intimacy until they were here.

The bar was closing and in the blink of an eye it was 2am. The time for reckoning was fast approaching and both of them knew it. They were ready. This was a long time in the making. Well, actually it wasn't really, not in the grand scheme of things. They'd only actually met each other four days before, but it felt a whole lot longer, especially as they'd openly declared they wanted to have sex together and were holding back until now.

They joked in the lift about how needing to wee could really throw a spanner in their careful planning. This would not play out like it did in the movies. Instead, while they considered this inconvenience (or convenience), they kissed intently on the ride down two floors. Lou was sure it would have made great viewing on the security cameras. Their desire was effervescing like steam rising above them as their tongues entwined. The lift mirrors helped to fuel the passion whilst their arms and legs wrapped around each other, ever trying to get in closer.

In the room Lou dashed straight into the toilet, so she was ready. Amos did the exactly the same as soon as she emerged. It was his time to prepare himself. Lou touched up her lipstick and then laid on the bed waiting for him. 'He'd better be good' Lou thought to herself and most fortunately she wasn't disappointed.

In fact Lou was delighted to discover that Amos was indeed a pleaser of women in the oral department and before long he had Lou wriggling all over that hotel room, starting with the king size bed. He was a tender lover who certainly paid attention to detail and how to make Lou feel at her very best. And whilst he spent ages licking, nibbling and sucking her most precious area, Lou surprisingly felt she just wasn't about to have that almighty crescendo fanfare explosion that she was so desperate to release. Something was holding her back and she couldn't quite put her finger on what it was that was causing the block. Maybe it was because actually, she didn't know him that well and didn't feel relaxed enough to let go? Could it be that the week at her relatively new employer had in fact caused more fatigue than she had realised? Or was it the gin? Possibly it was a combination of all those factors, but whatever it was, Lou knew she had to calm them all down so she could enjoy this moment in its entirety.

Lou's right hand wandered down to offer some assistance but Amos unexpectedly brushed it aside. (Lou found some men's idea of heaven was to have a woman play with herself when they were pleasuring her, but given the effort he had put in so far, Lou couldn't help but agree that he deserved this one all to himself.) She moved her hand to grabbing her thigh instead and let him continued with his quest to make her come.

A momentum was building now. Lou flitted from looking directly at him to looking up at the ceiling. She was beginning to relax more in the moment when he suddenly shouted: "Look at me Lou-Lou!" Ooh that certainly caught her attention instantly. She focused on watching him slowly licking her pussy. She had flickers of orgasm making an appearance now as she began to let her mind drift and the sensations wash over her. Ah yeah, there it was. It was hovering in the distance and would soon be within her grasp. It wouldn't be long at all and she was happy to share that with him. Lou could feel it was getting closer. "Just there; oh yeah... just there. Oh god yeah... Yeah, yeah, oh fuck yeah!" And there it was: simple as that. It was mind-blowingly awesome, as the waves of orgasm crashed all over Lou's body from the inside out, and spattering Amos at the same time. It was one of those massive earth-moving ones that made Lou crumple up and jitter all around the bed uncontrollably.

Now Amos was looking pleased with himself and quite deservedly too. He'd hit her jackpot and the prize was pouring out. In fact he did look a little startled when she began to gush. "Wow Lou-Lou. You squirt too?" Amos asked, looking a little sheepish and somewhat overwhelmed. "Only when stimulated enough," Lou explained, "and you've certainly done that!" The proud look returned on his face.

It took a while for Lou to calm down. Strong after-shocks reverberated throughout her body before she finally came to rest, not that Lou had any intention to rest. It was time to show Amos how she compared with whatever he had been imagining for the past few days. Lou wasn't about to disappoint him. He'd been nothing but charming since the moment their eyes met at Liverpool Street station. In fact he'd treated her like a princess, fulfilling all of her needs and more. Now it was his turn to be indulged and she couldn't wait to taste him.

"Lay yourself down now Amos. I want to devour you." That beaming smile returned as he complied. He was certainly ready for her and this was blatantly apparent from her first viewing of his naked form before her. His body was lean and the obvious six-pack was protruding quite naturally. 'Damn, he is fine,' she thought to herself. There was no morsel of fat on this body. It reminded her of a policeman she once had a relationship with, but the skin tone could not have contrasted any more. "Your body is amazing Amos," she told him. He was embarrassed but thanked her all the same. There was no need for him to be shy, not with the performance he had just put in on her nether regions. They were way beyond bashfulness now!

Kissing Amos was an exciting delight. Their tongues were like old friends who, once engaged, didn't want to stop their exhilarating interactions. It made them both incredibly horny and it was hard for Lou to prize herself away, but she had further destinations on her list. So she took her time making her way from his delicious mouth to his neck, which proved exceptionally sensitive. She knew exactly where she was heading, with some diversion across his chest and the down that washboard stomach to her prize. It was time now to work her magic on his cock and she wouldn't be holding back on her treatment of it.

Lou had her fair share of fit bodies and humongous penises over the past few years. She found there were benefits and negatives when it came to the size of the package. Some men claim they've got the biggest one women would ever have experienced and happily post pictures of them online for all to see. They even send them to people who really do not want to receive them, as Lou had experienced on various social media sites. Lou had blocked enough people on Facebook (of all places) for that over the past year or so. They were sent via Messenger, which has very different rules it seems to its host site.

Lou had previously been impressed when her friend Rebecca showed her how to spot the lesser cock, carefully placed in photographs for ample exposure and misperception!

Lou had also met quite a few gym-addicted guys who spent so much time exercising and trying to improve their bodies, that it just highlighted issues elsewhere. There were a whole host of insecurities to be found and Lou appreciated it was good to have some sort of healthy balance. (This didn't mean she would date fat men. The more lean variety was her preference and she was entitled to have what she liked!)

Lou looked in wonder at the different skin coloration as she just about managed to consume his penis whole. It ranged from dark brown to a lighter pink in some places. It was quite the work of art! As it reached the back of her throat, Lou didn't gag but continued her devouring. She stroked the throbbing tip back and forth with her tongue while cupping his balls. He liked that. His sighing had increased in volume, as had his deeper breathing. She maintained eye contact throughout. It was rather horny to watch his different reactions, ranging from pure delight, to intensity that was possibly becoming unbearably tingly, back to bliss once more. His smiling face was looking down at her as she continued to pleasure him. "Damn Lou-Lou, I want you." It was more of a pleading and for Lou the feeling was completely mutual. She couldn't wait to ride him. The desire was at an all-time high and needed to be nourished.

Both of them had brought condoms and no awkward conversation or explaining was necessary. Amos reached to his wash bag next to the bed and swiftly adorned the protection. It meant Lou could straddle him and ease herself gently down: all the while with their eyes interlocked as before. "Parfait Lou-Lou!" His accent was incredibly sexy, if a little cliché. She loved listening to him speak French, or English for that matter. It all sounded divine to her and was certainly adding to the mood.

Given this was their first session together, and how they had patiently waited those extra days for it, they chose to try every position and every counter in their hotel room. The mirrored bathroom was a particular favourite as they watched themselves from different angles, eventually making their way back to the semi-sodden bed they had desecrated earlier. This would be a long and naughty night! Bearing in mind they had been at work all day, caught a plane to Spain, drank at the alfresco bar and then continued on to enjoy this physical treat, Lou did wonder where on earth all that energy came from? It was quite remarkable really how you could continue going when you were enjoying yourself so much!

Eventually this spent pair did seek solace in their separate sides of the bed and soon they rested. Amos was delighted to find that any waking moments were met with the reciprocal response he had hoped for. Lou was not in the habit of rolling over or protesting if her partner woke up with desire on his mind. She was only too pleased to oblige. Her hunger was usually on par and sometimes more ravenous than those who woke up with her. 'Why would you waste it? If you were there to have sex with someone you fancied, then why not take every opportunity to do so!' Lou thought to herself. It really was as simple as that!

With the intermittent play that continued, it invariably meant that breakfast would be missed. Even though it was included in the hotel deal, as with many hotel stays, Lou found she often missed the sitting. This was never a problem, despite her loving the most important meal of the day. Today they would find something to eat elsewhere. Instead they had shared a delectable start the day, which was delectable in its own way, and Amos certainly wasn't complaining!

Once they had finished a further round of the hotel room, they showered and got ready to go out. They were ravenous now and being beach-bound, that was where they would find some sustenance. The sun was beating down on them and Lou was in her element. She loved the sunshine and could happily bake in it all day.

What a perfect mystery weekend this was turning out to be. Amos was the perfect gent and the pair found themselves chatting and laughing all day, all weekend in fact. This escapade was a gamble for them both: to spend that much time with someone you have just met and hardly know at all, but Lou's instincts were right. It was a risk she did not regret taking and it certainly paid off!

Chapter 8 - Attempt two at the submissive

When life took a different turn for a certain dominant acquaintance of hers, Lou looked to explore an alternative side of herself with someone else. What a shame: Lou had psyched herself up to indulge in the submissive, just to see what it was really like. It was not that she particularly wanted to adopt that kink. That was not her thing at all and it didn't feel natural in the slightest. If anything, Lou had more dominant tendencies, as she had recently discovered (*see Cinnamon Twist*). But in order to pursue that side with more confidence, Lou thought it would be beneficial to experience both submissive and dominant traits to fully understand and appreciate them.

Lou had friends who felt truly complete with crop marks and bruises across their buttocks. They also had to ask their Master if they were allowed to go to parties and if so, who could they sleep with when there, if anyone? What could they wear? What time should they return home, and so on and so forth? Lou found it difficult to get her head around such behaviour, but she wanted to. In her exploration of all things sexual, she recognised there was obviously something in it that people enjoyed. This was made a little clearer to her when a very strong-minded female friend of hers told her how refreshing it was not to have to think for herself. There was no dilemma now in decision-making. Her Master took that responsibility away and she was left with the easier task of following orders instead. This kind of made more sense, but again it was totally alien to Lou.

Lou was only too delighted to hear from her very old friend and ex-work colleague 'Rock Hunter' (and we'll call him Rock from hereon. Talk about a bloody mouthful ha ha!) They had kept in touch for years as he relocated on a number of occasions with work. It seemed he was on his own journey of discovery too and since she had known him, he'd gone from her potential lover to a sharer of all kinkier paraphernalia. Lou used to choose (over Skype) the 'gadget' she wanted him to use on himself from the various implements he lined up for her to select from. He was halfway around the world and he would film putting the tool in place, as he came for her in real time – usually over a printed copy of one of her photographs.

From sex toys to prostitutes to eventually getting married, Rock lived a very secret life: one that only Lou and his paid associates were privy to. They remained friends despite the miles and when she divorced and relocated, Rock very generously sent her a moving in present that was not of the usual kind. There was no 'new home' card, not a pot plant or flowers. Instead it consisted of a vibrating butt plug, anal lubricant, a 'strapless strap-on' and a lace Teddy outfit. It was very far from the routine gift, but then again, so was their relationship.

Some four years had passed since then and still their exchanges continued. These were more of the kind explaining what they had individually experienced of late, invariably ending with Rock again filming himself coming over Lou's picture. For him, there was pleasure to be taken by smothering a naughty photo in semen and watching it sink into Lou's body (or actually into the paper as it absorbed the moisture). For her it was more about listening to his sighs and gasps whilst knowing he was utterly focussing on her image while completing the release. This happened a few times before he moved back to the UK (and in with his new wife), where this activity ceased.

Rock told Lou he had a submissive (sub) he regularly met with and was 'showing her the ropes' both practically and metaphorically. Having gained her permission, his sub (whom he called his Slave) agreed for him to show Lou her pictures and he happily shared this 45 year old blonde in his requested outfits and poses. He explained how she had only recently got in touch with this side of her life, having just come out of a love-less partnership. Rock was educating her in ways she was hungry for and couldn't get enough apparently. It seemed that both of them were getting exactly what they needed from this set up, but Rock wanted more. As he was already in a suppressed marriage, he was looking for more from his Slave and whilst she was keen, he wanted to drive this relationship to an all new level of depravity, although was conscious to work at an agreed pace with her.

Lou had known Rock for years as a sub himself, so it was interesting for her to hear about him being the dom (dominant) in this relationship. She couldn't imagine him being the Master, although this ability to 'switch' seemed to hit all of his buttons. He could go from being the one in control at the office, managing vast numbers of people and responsible for many IT systems, to become the one being told what to do – and quite forcefully too. The Rock Lou knew had been paying for women to take control of his world at least one afternoon per month. Most of the recent times he would pay for two to visit him at once. And now he was the one giving out orders? This was new territory and one that sparked some interest for Lou.

Lou was curious to learn how he had swapped from sub to dom and which he preferred of the two, or did it depend on the mood? As suspected, Rock told her he enjoyed both, and was very keen to take up the role of Lou's new Master, should she still want to progress this line of experience. Equally, he was interested to know if Lou would like to be part of a forthcoming photo shoot, where she would be his Mistress and he would be her Slave for some very erotic storytelling? This was a chance for Lou to be in front of the camera, in raunchy outfits and being the centre of attention? How could she resist?

Rock set it all up and the plan was to use the discreet garage he rented quite close to his home in Colchester. It was set up as a playroom with various items of 'furniture' in place for his pleasure. This included a wall-mounted wooden cross (more like an X than a crucifix-type cross), spanking chair, gym jump horse and sex swing, along with various tools and toys hanging from the rafters and on shelves. There was even a bar area, with stools, which he had used to entertain and relax guests in the past.

When Lou arrived, she took a while to marvel at his collection. It really was quite impressive and must have cost him a fortune! She was also pleased to see sanitizer sprays, clothes, wipes, bags and condoms at the ready, and the detergent smell was apparent as she walked in.

His friend Greg was a photographer who was only too pleased to be part of this BDSM shoot. He had carried them out before for Rock and Lou suspected these two men had shared more than camera frames during those experiences! They were certainly very comfortable in each other's company and they made Lou feel at ease instantly. It was initially a little strange for Lou because she had actually known Rock for some fifteen years now, but had never actually seen him in the flesh under such circumstances. Admittedly she'd seen most of him in some guise or lucrative position over those years, but never quite standing (or squatting) in person nor right in front of her. She hoped this wouldn't affect their friendship, but given all they had been through already, that was highly unlikely.

Rock had described the contents of the trunk he kept at the site. It was full to bursting of latex, leather and PVC outfits, which Lou was welcomed to sift through and find some items to wear for the shoot. When Lou came to delve in this box of goodies, it was clear that some garments were for his own use, as the dresses and stockings were way too big for a woman of Lou's size, not to mention the photos he had sent her over the years of him dressed as a female. Rock had told her not to bother bringing any of her own outfits as he had plenty, which was apparent now, but she had packed her latex cat suit and 6" patent heels, just in case. It was just as well too, as most of the shoes he had in stock were either size 5, which were slightly too small for Lou, or size 11, which was obviously his size!

As Lou had come to expect, his planning was meticulous. (No wonder he needed this form of relief from time to time!) He had prepared a script, which she had run through the week before, and was up to speed on what he wanted to achieve in this shoot. Primarily it was for his own purposes, but what he wanted to portray was that 'normal' people can enjoy a bit of BDSM fun just as much as anyone else. He was tired of people thinking those who enjoy a bit of kink were all perverts or weirdos when in fact it was perfectly healthy and fun to have this kind of release, even if it was a little different perhaps to what they chose to explore as good-hearted entertainment! It was funny actually because Lou wanted people to know exactly the same about swingers too!

Where Rock was more established in the BDSM world, he was keen for Lou to understand that it wasn't just about sex and orgasms. It was about the planning and the build up to the actual play session. Lou knew exactly what he was describing as she had teased many men along her own journey, but this was usually a manner of days or weeks. There had been exceptions where the period ahead of play had been longer in the making, where mental as well as physical teasing took place, meaning it was quite a relief to actually get to be living out the fantasy together when the act finally happened.

Rock described how he loved to give his Slave all the pleasure she (or he) could take. The build-up ahead of assembling was a time to reveal their darkest secrets, in the safety of their shared arrangement, and for them to feel comfortable exploring them in person should they wish to when they met. The initial apprehension was lost as the confidence grew, as they either engaged utterly to take control of Rock, or they submitted to his control and played out the fantasy of being his to tantalise. The mental release in this type of session was far stronger than the physical orgasm and this was something Lou was keen to explore from either perspective, but for this time as the Mistress.

Lou had noted that during the course of the photography that this would play out as a normal dom/sub session and the usual rules of no sex would apply (as in no fucking). Equally, the high standards of hygiene and safety would be maintained. There would be clear communications on limits and boundaries, so there was no confusion on either side. That sounded perfectly reasonable to Lou – all very sensible in fact.

This was the usual course of events, however, as the shooting was to continue, Lou noted that, should she so desire, the photographs Rock wished to achieve would lead to her simulating a demand that he eat her pussy, as indeed she would later instruct him to lick his cum off her tits, bum or shoes. It was optional for her to choose whether she wanted him to penetrate her and she hadn't quite decided yet if she would pursue that. As it was, this was the first time they had actually been together in a room for many years, and they had never shared any fluids other than a couple of kisses a lifetime ago. The beauty and the longevity of their relationship were probably based upon this unknowing of pleasures shared. With this line being crossed, it could end it dead. If either of them failed to live up to the anticipated and much deliberated levels of passion, then it would be over in an instant! They had joked in the past that this was the longest foreplay either of them had ever experienced, so would it be risky to go any further or should they maintain their not knowing?

Lou had put it out of her mind for now and told Rock she would decide on the day, which had come around all too fast! She was a little nervous herself as to how this would play out, but she felt a little more comfortable now, given how relaxed both men were, even if the adrenalin was surging through her body!

With the script agreed and the cameras set up, it was time to change into their outfits. That was easy for Rock. He was laughing as he cheekily revealed he was already dressed! Underneath his somewhat baggy jeans, he showed them he was already prepared, with his cock locked securely in its cage, trapped inside some leather pants! "Oh right – so you've started ahead of me I see!" Lou joked, almost wanting to set the scene of this slightly different liaison than normal. It was fine. They were all pretty chilled and jovial. After all, they were in this mission together, to achieve some new art, even if it did teeter on the more erotic side of photography! Rock tended to the music to accompany their mood. AC/DC was the order of the day and a good choice they all agreed!

Lou took another look through the box of outfits. Given she was the Mistress, she fully intended on wearing her own shiny latex cat suit, but there was no harm in seeing what else he had in there to choose from. There was an abundance of paraphernalia Lou could really have some fun with, if she had the trunk to herself for a week or maybe three! But the chaps were keen to get moving, so she opted for her original attire. As usual it was difficult to peel the rubber onto her body, even with the additional lubricant she applied to her skin ahead of the task. Rock offered to help, but then admitted he would be of absolutely no use whatsoever. He was only too familiar with the limitations of latex and it was just best to persevere by herself, which she did! Finally in place, she grabbed those beautiful shoes she had brought with her. They were so high that she had to remain seated to do the buckles up otherwise she was bound to wobble over! Once firmly in place, she raised herself up and found that she was only 8" shorter than Rock now, despite her instant growth in height!

The first images were to be of Rock with his collar in place and Lou's hand firmly on the chain. He was to be kneeling in front of her, whilst she sat at one of the bar stools looking down at him. His face would depict utter adoration as he intently looked at her and then kissed the top of her shoe. Surprisingly for Lou, both pictures were very easy to take, as the lighting had been put in place earlier at this scene. Greg stood above her left shoulder and pointed his camera down at Rock. He made minor adjustments to his lights before he was happy with the results and showed them to them both. Rock's face lit up immediately as he became aware he was really achieving what he had set out to do. "I can't believe we are actually doing this. I've wanted to bring this to life for so long!" Lou was thrilled for him too and it really was quite effortless! What Lou was quite surprised about was that despite depicting BDSM scenes, this wasn't turning her on in the slightest! She appeared to have conducted her own switch for this moment – from friend to professional model!

The next planned scenario Lou had refused to do ahead of this day. Whilst she was game for most things, this wasn't one of them and Rock reluctantly agreed, but only because he could have been harmed in the process! On the scale of perverse, this probably wasn't mentioned, but on the ticklish scale, it was through the roof for Lou! There was no way she could physically let him kneel down in front of her and kiss and lick her toes! She just couldn't do it! Sod the subservient looking up at her – there was no way she could sit there and take it: not without kicking him in the face, which he just might not appreciate (or maybe he would)?

Now wearing a black rubber strap-on was a different story. They moved to the centre of the room and Greg adjusted the lighting. Lou was happy to oblige as she stepped into the harness and held the 'penis' in one hand as Rock crouched below her and licked the tip. Again Greg stood above her, so the shot showed Rock looking upwards. Lou sensed something between them. They were both enjoying this particular visual just a little too much. "Are you sure you don't want to put this on instead Greg?" Lou mused and a few sniggers followed from them both. 'Naughty boys,' Lou thought! A few more takes in this position and both gentlemen were satisfied with the result, before Rock then began to then suck the strap-on instead for a different image, which Greg captured before they moved on.

The pictures to create now were about the Mistress receiving oral pleasure and to simulate the Slave obeying his mistress's need to be fulfilled. This is where Lou thought she might have a little flutter down there in her rubber! She sat on the stool once more and unzipped her cat suit from the groin zip to the bum, so her pussy was now exposed. She had specifically requested that there were no upwards shots taken of her legs spread apart, as she wished to keep this private, however, downward shots were permitted.

Lou placed her hands on her thighs and threw her head back. Rock's instruction was to be photographed leaning towards her with his tongue outstretched. (Secretly Lou wanted him to take her there and then, particularly as she could feel the heat of his tongue, but she was keeping it professional. Perhaps at the end of the session there would be time for play – should she so desire. She was the Mistress after all and she'd wanted to have a bi-male threesome for many years!)

Once captured, the next was for Lou to be standing up straight, with her legs either side of Rock's face. The intention was to show him feasting on her, or at least appearing to be, again shot from above. This was easy to achieve as Lou slightly squatted to meet his tongue, or rather made it look that way to the viewer. It was killing her inside not to just drop down on him and let him have his way, but she maintained her control. This session was becoming way more about teasing and build up than she had ever imagined it would be! She wondered if Rock had known that all along? If he had, he was certainly keeping quiet about it now!

The final shot for Lou was to show her booting him out of the room. She was finished with his services and it was time for him to leave. (They would put them in sequence after the shoot, but for clothing reasons, this would be pictured next.) Rock knelt on the floor, heading for the open doorway, with Lou's heel firmly on his buttock, shoving him out. Lou may have dug her heel in just a little bit more than required for the camera and Rock gasped in response. He turned and threw her a cheeky smile. "Oh it's like that is it Mistress?" She smiled and asked, "Did I say you could address me?" Nothing wrong with a little role-play after all, particularly in these circumstances!

The next series of pictures were more about Rock's subservience, with whipping and spanking marks to be shown on his bottom. Having removed his shorts, Lou helped Greg to tie Rock's leather cuffs on his wrists and ankles and then attach him to the cross. Once in place Lou then went about warming up his skin. She was aware that it could be painful and unpleasant to start with force straight away. It was better to swipe, rub the skin to help it acclimatise and then to continue, which is what she proceeded to do, with Greg taking a number of action shots along the way. She had a variety of canes and paddles to use on him with different degrees of contact, which he looked to be thoroughly enjoying!

When Rock was removed from the cross, she noticed that his cock had swollen in the process and was desperately trying to escape the cage. He was in a subdued state, almost trancelike as he managed the uncomfortable scenario. He longed for nothing more than to be released and this made for another, unplanned photograph. Lou made him kneel in front of her, with the key to release him dangling on the end of a cane in front of him. Greg was soon to capture the image from behind where she stood. Rock's face needed no guidance. The relief he sought was obvious and beautifully immortalised on camera.

Finally were the shots Lou had now come to slightly dread, but it was necessary to finalise this sequence. She knew Rock needed to cum. It was written all over his face and she was not prepared to deny him this pleasure. What she didn't want was for him to fuck her. Quite far from it in fact as she had become a little put off by the last scene that had played out. It wasn't the spanking or whipping, but his weary face and his need for relief. She saw him as pitiful and weak, and it had put her off a little bit.

"Where am I allowed to cum Mistress?" he asked her innocently. Remaining in character, she said "You may cum on my shoes and you must lick them clean afterwards." Rock and Lou had previously discussed this act. Under direction and whilst observing his Mistress, he would gladly drink his own semen, but only because that was her desire. Under normal circumstances this would repulse him. On the other hand, today for the camera, he would do as she instructed, and Greg caught the moment for posterity.

The photo shoot was now complete and they reflected on the day's events, as they returned to their usual roles! Lou stepped out of her shoes carefully and handed them to Rock, who was only too keen to carefully clean them as instructed. Her cat suit was filled with sweat and easily poured off her body as she removed it. She didn't mind the two guys watching this. They'd seen her pussy and compromising positions, so seeing her naked really wasn't an issue. Without a shower or sink, Lou had to make do with the copious wipes Rock had for that very purpose.

Greg promised to have the images ready for review by the end of the week and would send them to Rock, as usual. Lou was eager to view them on a larger screen than his camera, so she could see them in detail, and have her own record of the day. Rock promised he wouldn't circulate any without her express permission, and given their friendship and trust, she knew he would be true to his word.

It had been an altogether very different experience for Lou. It wasn't quite the sub/dom exploration she had wanted to get an understanding of, although it had opened her eyes to both sides of that BDSM world and she understood the release better - both mentally and physically. However people chose to relieve themselves (albeit legally), she was acceptable of and had no reason to judge people differently just because they played out fantasies in a way she couldn't quite connect with.

The next outing with Rock would be one of the original request: for him to be her Master and her his Slave. How they could ever actually achieve that, she did wonder, but who knows eh? 'Never say never,' Lou thought!

Chapter 9 - Party time

A number of her friends had mentioned Charlotte's parties, but Lou hadn't made it to one yet. They normally fell on the Saturday nights when she had her children and given they were on a set rotation, she was never likely to go to one either. The same applied to a number of other organized events that fell on the same nights, where Lou's children would always take precedence over her social life. So when Charlotte announced a weekday rendezvous at a new London location, Lou was excited to confirm that, as it fell on a childfree school night, she was definitely up for it! The decision now was as to who she would like her party partner to be...

Being on a Thursday and in the City, there were a number of potential guys Lou could choose to join her. They would have to be approved by the host, with photographic evidence, which meant the standard of other attendees would be high too. This always made for a good night. Now you could call Lou shallow, but she liked quality people in both the looks as well as intelligence departments! The latter you couldn't always guarantee, but sometimes it was a price she was willing to pay!

Lorenzo was her first choice. She'd met him at a fetish event some months before and hadn't spoken to him for a while, but given he'd previously mentioned wanting to go to one of Charlotte's parties; he was the obvious choice. He was also based in Greenwich, so it wouldn't be far for him to travel and Lou was sure he'd offer for her to stay with him afterwards if she wanted to. This would make it easy for her to get to work too the next day.

Lorenzo was certainly a gent and Lou was thrilled when he confirmed his availability. "I would be delighted to accompany you beautiful Lou." She loved Italians. So blatantly charming, even when they knew they were already on a promise! There was no need to woo her, but still he did and she liked that. Lou loved attention – she always had. They would definitely be having sex together and possibly with a few other people too. Who knew? They would see how the party panned out and who else attended.

It was a mediocre day in the office, with Lou's attention elsewhere for most of it. She completed the work she needed to do but her focus was really on the forthcoming passionate evening that was lined up. In her trusted small black rucksack was her makeup and clothes: little black dress for the evening and crease-free wrap dress for the office tomorrow. The heels she wore for work would suffice for the party, as they were 4" any way and accentuated her calf muscles gloriously. Spare knickers and hold ups for tomorrow were packed and a sheer corset for naughtiness later. Lou's minimal makeup was onboard too and once her office day drew to a close, she carefully applied that at the work gym downstairs post-showering. Now she was fresh as a daisy and about to get dirty!

Lorenzo suggested a Turkish restaurant close to the swanky hotel that overlooked the 'Gherkin' office block.

They met at 6.30pm and spent the next two hours catching up, flirting and nourishing themselves ahead of any activity. Making sure they didn't overfill themselves, they kept the meal light and enjoyed a bottle of Sauvignon Blanc before walking ten minutes to the venue, stopping off at the local express supermarket for a bottle of Prosecco to take with them.

They had not been told the room number yet, but that came through as a text while they sat at the hotel bar. A gin and tonic was in order ahead of whatever was in store - which could never quite be guaranteed with these nights. With both of them being first timers to this particular event, they were a little nervous as to what to expect, but given the reviews, Lou was sure they'd have a most sexy and memorable night. At worst, they'd end up back at his enjoying each other, which was inevitable one way or another, and would be worth it too, given their previous naked encounter.

With their glasses emptied, a quick check reiterated that they had their bottle, condoms and themselves, so they ventured to the lift area. The 14th floor was their destination and the message had requested they be respectful and discreet. The hotel was unaware a sex party was being hosted in one of their suites and the intention was to keep it that way! It would be devastating if the management caught wind of it and threw the organisers out. (Although Lou's favourite swinging club was just around the corner, if all else failed. She was incredibly resourceful after all!)

Another couple had exited the bar at the same moment they did and the four of them were now waiting for the lift. It was obvious to Lou they were going to the same place. The wine bottle in hand gave it away, as well as the glamorously dressed attire, which could have been appropriate for any occasion really, but there was an air of mischief about them, which Lou picked up on immediately. "Room 1459 is it?" she said with a presumptuous smile on her face. The couple in unison sheepishly nodded their heads and laughed. "Was it that obvious?" The blond, forty-something lady asked Lou. Lou smiled and agreed as they struck up further conversation while the lift took them to their destination of depravity. The other couple had attended a few of the weekend parties prior to tonight and were complimentary, but were unsure if a weekday version would be quite as exhilarating. All would soon be revealed - literally!

The foursome approached room 1459 together and rang the suite's bell. An attractive South African guy answered, dressed in smart trousers, light blue shirt and muscles a-bulging! 'Hello' Lou thought and also said aloud but for very different purposes. He was so her type. She wondered if he was on the menu tonight, but that would have to wait. There was some admin to do first. They had to get themselves ticked off the guest list, store their coats and Lorenzo paid their 'couples' entry fee. Now they were good to go. Time to get circulating, check out the facilities and to see who else was on offer.

Lou was pleasantly surprised to find she knew two ladies in the main lounge area. They were her fellow 'Flavas' from days gone by (*see Vanilla Extract*) and they had shared many a man and many a steamy night at various locations. The last time their paths had crossed was at a rugby after-party some six months before and that had certainly been an eventful evening. You can imagine the girly screams and hugs that then ensued as they became reacquainted. None of them had realised each other were planning on attending Charlotte's party, so that was an even more unexpected coincidence (*which Lou didn't ever believe in, as avid readers will know*). A few selfies were taken while the clothes were still on to send to their missing Flava member Lucy, and then their phones were put away, to comply with the event's privacy rules, which were entirely appropriate given the nature of the party.

Next the ladies' partners were introduced, as they had somewhat been forgotten when the reunion commenced. Lou didn't know any of them, which made it interesting, although Rebecca's choice of man always struck Lou as somewhat suspect. Tonight she had brought a very handsome, strapping, bald black gentleman with her, who Lou thought had potential. (Lou recalled one guy that she and Lucy had joked about looking like he'd just got off his tractor at a previous event. Whilst Lou could attest firsthand there was absolutely nothing wrong with farmers, he could have at least got changed and showered before he came out!)

Sabrina'a partner was not really one for Lou. She had a thing about older men, like seriously older, and that just didn't do it for Lou. Why not have the older man when she was older too? That seemed to make more sense to her, at this stage in her life any way. Lorenzo was 41 and had the body of someone ten years younger. He had enough worldly experience and independence too to hold a decent conversation and the banter to match Lou's.

Scouting around the room now, Lou saw four other

couples and two single females. It was time to take a tour of the suite for later use and then work the room to meet some new people. The facilities were very similar to a West End venue she'd partied at before: two en-suite bedrooms, one larger than the other, and a lounge area with adjoining kitchen. Drinks and nibbles were conveniently placed in the latter, whilst other essentials, namely condoms, were dotted about in all rooms.

Lorenzo followed by her side and was equally as chatty when they introduced themselves to the other guests. This was the time where Lou sized up the other people, as did everyone else, and made a mental note of whom she would like to play with during the course of the evening. For now, apart from her party partner, there were two additional men in her potential 'to do' list! Whilst the others there looked fun, she doubted there would be any further involvement when it came to the group play, although she wouldn't rule it out just yet. In the heat of the moment, who knew what new discoveries would be made?

One of the single ladies Lou had met many times before. She usually hung around in another cliquey group that rocked up to various locations Lou had frequented. Lou had been an honorary member of that group for a while, but decided she didn't want to be self-restrictive by associating with only one network. As a free spirit she enjoyed moving from circle to circle as and when she wanted and with no demands on her constantly being with the same people. Lou was and always had been her own person. That was very unlikely to change unless 'the one' came along, for whatever that was worth!

Nevertheless, it was good to see Lana again. Some

reminiscing began there too and Lou couldn't help feeling it was a night to rekindle friendships as well as throw caution to the wind and have a jolly good fucking! Lana asked after a mutual previous partner whom she had fallen out with. Lou hadn't seen him since the last time they'd gone to Le Boudoir, where she vowed she would never have sex with him again. This sparked Lana's interest. "Oh, why is that? Did he upset you?" Lou went on to tell her the story as to why she was now abstaining from him, despite his most awesome physique and most ride-able cock. In a moment on the huge shared bed space, he was thrusting away at her and throughout the moment, he was eyeing up his next conquest. Now this alone wouldn't really have made much difference to Lou, as she was guilty of the same, but given she was about to climax, you know: a special shared moment, she thought the least he could do was watch her come! That was just bad manners in Lou's opinion! Therein laid the reason she would not be revisiting him or his delightful penis!

Lana had eagerly listened to Lou's story and then relayed her own. This was not so much about diverted attention but the need he had to surround himself with girls younger than Lou's eldest daughter. Not only that, but he felt the need to have two in tow. This was definitely an ego trip about proving he could still attract beautiful women. The fact they took the piss out of his generosity seemed to go unnoticed, but that was up to him. Lana has tried to discuss it with him, but he took offence and they had since not spoken. Lou could relate. She'd seen him at a party recently and he'd bragged about the women he'd brought along: one was 21 and the other 23. They were replicas of his previous long-term

110

girlfriend, which was a little unnerving too. They paid him little attention there but had happily been wined and dined beforehand. Maybe he was their sugar daddy? He was over 30 years older after all. Who knew? Lou wasn't here to judge. That was his choice and Lou hoped it was bringing him whatever it was he needed, although she suspected it only provided the short term high.

It was almost 10pm now and guests were beginning to loosen up a little. More alcohol was consumed and the volume of chatting had increased. The bright lights had been dimmed and the atmosphere was becoming more relaxed. No one else had shown up since they arrived and according to the guest list, just one other couple had booked, but had messaged to say they been let down by their childminder.

'It's time to get this show on the road," Lou thought to herself, as she lifted her dress over her head and off, revealing that all so sexy see-through lingerie. It was the cue to get things started, as if everyone else had been waiting for some sort of signal. Lou had provided the trigger they needed, as the rest of the female contingent began to follow suit. Some men also began to unbutton shirts, but others were a little more reluctant, initially that is.

Lorenzo was standing in front of Lou in the middle of the room, as she began to unbutton his shirt for him. At the same time she slipped her tongue in his mouth and his right hand immediately came up and grabbed her back and brought her closer to him. This instantly sent tingles throughout her body. She absolutely adored it when a man did that. It demonstrated the passion flowing intensely and that sense of togetherness, as they were bonded by their mouths and gripping on with intent. Her super sensitive neck also thrived on the hand moving up to hold her head in place as he devoured her tongue. That was so hot!

Breaking away, Lou dropped to her knees. It was time to continue this show. She carefully positioned her feet under her, so her heels were placed comfortably on the thick carpet, before she unbuttoned his trousers purposely slowly. She had an audience to entertain after all!

His trousers fell to the ground and now she was faced with his bright white Calvin Klein pants, which fit him perfectly (*unlike Pants in Vanilla Extract*). They were beginning to become a little tight for Lorenzo, as his trapped bulge began to pulsate before her. It wasn't difficult to work out what Lou had planned for next, as she reached into his underwear, scooped up a hold of his growing organ and released his beast into the open. The pants quickly joined his trousers on the floor and Lou began to gorge herself on him.

Lorenzo only looked down at the start of this encounter and then a couple of times during this treat. His focus was mainly on the ceiling or with his eyes closed. He paid no attention to the other guests who were enjoying the spectacle but had not yet begun to pleasure themselves. It appeared their voyeuristic tendencies had come into play momentarily.

Lou continuously looked up at him, absorbing every sigh and gasp as she devotedly pleasured him. She was aware of the spectators' attention as it burned into the back of her. This just fuelled her desire to make this the best blowjob they'd ever witnessed. A cheeky turn around confirmed it was working! All eyes were on them both, which is exactly what she enjoyed. This gave her a sense of control as well as adoration. (*She attributed this to her childhood need for attention and to be shown love by the first adult man in her life. Counselling paid for that revelation when Lou had previously enquired as to whether she was a sex addict!*) For now, she enjoyed working her magic.

Lorenzo was leaking slightly but Lou didn't want him to come yet. She had tenderly caressed his entire groin with her tongue and intermittently taken his entire shaft fully down her throat. She had allowed his pre-come to flow freely as she licked it up, but he was most definitely not allowed to ejaculate yet. The edge was just where she wanted him, before she called a halt to the hot demonstration. Now it was time to turn the tables. "It's time for the bedroom Lorenzo. I want you deep inside me. Let's go." His face displayed mixed emotions as his bliss was interrupted, but he knew it wouldn't be long before it recommenced next door.

From kneeling, Lou stood up, and with her hands either side of him she brought his clothes up with her. 'Ever-practical eh?' She thought to herself. It was almost like she had done that before ha! As Lorenzo held the clothes against his waist with his right hand, Lou picked up her dress and led him with his left to the larger bedroom. She could hear behind her that others were intending on joining them, as drinks were abandoned in the kitchen area. The chink of many glasses on marble confirmed the exodus.

Lorenzo removed all of his clothes this time, folded them carefully and placed them and Lou's dress to the side of the bed on the floor. 'How very house-trained'

113

Lou thought as he motioned for her to lay down and was soon devouring her moist pussy. It seemed the show had given her quite a thrill and certainly got her juices flowing. Lou was lying back with her eyes closed, feet still on the floor. She wanted to feel every lick of her clitoris, both around and across it: to savour each slide of the tongue inside her vagina and out, and the tingle of him nibbling her thighs. Then came his fingers to accompany the sensitive melody he'd begun to strum. The intensity of his playing was building her orgasm and Lou was riding every wave he created. Her legs were now up in the air and before she knew it the gushing began. The speed and depth of his fingers was saturating the bed as she uncontrollably squirted. Lou wondered if Lorenzo had planned to have her soak the side of the bed? It was very practical if he had, given many more people would be fucking on it momentarily. There was nothing worse than laying in someone else's damp patch when you were just starting your own fun: well that's what Lou thought anyway. There was probably someone out there that did like it, given the number and variety of different kinks people had!

Whilst Lou enjoyed the powerful squirt, it was a 'proper' orgasm she wanted with the fanfare ending. Lorenzo was still continuing his quest, and would happily have had her soaking the floor and the apartment below too, so she asked him to cease it. He immediately fingered her in the more traditional manner, whilst sucking and licking her all over. He obviously didn't mind this new more acidic flavour that smothered her swollen mound. Lou licked two fingers of her right hand and placed them either side of her clit. She was quite keen for some manual

114

intervention to move this along and Lorenzo was only too happy to watch while he finger fucked her. "So sexy, Lou," he murmured from down there! She certainly felt it!

Rubbing either side and across her fully charged button, the sensation was escalating. It was engulfing her entire body and it wouldn't be long before she blew! Greater and greater the waves grew in intensity, with her hips circulating to the rhythm of his fingers and hers. This duet worked perfectly in time and the crescendo was coming. "Oh fuck yes, yes. I'm so close," Lou screamed in delight. Her hips were raised now to feel every thrust and stroke even deeper. This was building rapidly. "Fuck. Yes. Oh god. Yes. Fuck. Fuck. Fuck. Oh yeah. Here we go. Fuck. FUCK YES!" She unashamedly shrieked. The volume had whacked up and there it was in full Dolby surround! Gasping repeatedly as she came, and completely forgetting where or who she was with, the ecstasy took hold of her and she was floating on air. 'Holy fuck that was a big one,' Lou thought as she started her gradual descent back to reality. 'Oh my god, that was so so good! Bloody hell I needed that!'

Lou had been too distracted to take any notice of anyone else. Once 'back in the room' she saw that the majority of other attendees were in various states of copulation. She'd felt that others were on the bed with her, but she had been too lost in her own orgasm development until now to pay any attention.

To her surprise, the South African host was to her right and was enjoying receiving a blowjob from Lana, who was sporting some very sexy underwear. "That was fucking hot," he told Lou. "Phew! Tell me about it," she laughed and puffed out air. Lana smiled up at her from his cock and signaled for Lou to share the meal. Meanwhile, with condom in place, Lorenzo had his hands on Lou's hips and wanted her to turn over and pound her from behind. With a little careful maneuvering, this could work out just right.

Lou swiveled over onto her knees, moved up the bed slightly (closely accompanied by Lorenzo) and at the very moment he slid his very patient cock inside her pussy, a South African cock was slipping in her mouth. Whilst still tingling from her own utopia, she was now being spit roasted and loving every sensation. 'Perfect!' Lou thought to herself as she and Lana took it in turns to deep throat, in between kissing each other and giggling. Tonight was proving quite the adventurous night: just what these parties should be!

Lou and Lorenzo did take a cab back to his Greenwich pad, but both were too spent to do much else that evening. They were pleased with how the night had gone and were certainly up for going to any more of Charlotte's weekday parties in the future.

Chapter 10 - It takes all sorts

Pride is a celebration of diversity, liberation and self-expression and while you can see the parade and enjoy the parties, you will never exhaust yourself of the creativity and openness involved. Lou wandered across the Gran Canaria dunes from her apartment to the beach on the morning of Sunday 11th November. At 11:11 at kiosk seven, the champagne and cava bottles would be popped and the partying become even crazier. There were always so many beautiful sights to behold as the costumes came to life and Lou appreciated just how much effort had gone into making the elaborate ensembles.

At the time of booking this trip, Lou knew it was Winter Pride. She also knew the German birthday gang would be in town, as they were on an annual basis, and being an honorary member of that group, Lou would no doubt see them at the beach or at a club. She was becoming quite a regular herself to the island and at various times of the year. Fortunately this meant she would always bump into people she had met on previous visits whenever she arrived at the more heterosexual kiosk number four.

The gay beach was filled to the brim with decorated people in groups with matching outfits and photos were taken left, right and centre of the various spectacles, by each other and the visiting onlookers. Lou soaked up the usual the party atmosphere which was fun-packed and alcohol-fuelled, with everyone laughing, hugging and generally messing around. Once she'd had her fill, she made her way along the shore to the area she normally frequented. Even that was busy, given the weather was particularly sunny and calm, plus you could get served quicker here than the other incredibly congested bar.

Lou wasn't ready for a drink yet. She'd had a skin-full the night before and whilst she wasn't feeling fragile, the thought of more alcohol this early wasn't doing it for her. No doubt it would after baking in the glorious sunshine that beheld her. With this being her last full day here, she was determined to work on her tan, even if it did get chilly when the clouds passed over.

Laying there, soaking up the rays, Lou thoroughly enjoyed being the single female on the beach. With her eyes closed, she often listened to the conversations of others without them taking much notice of her. Listening to English speakers, she was just being nosey: an audio voyeur as such. For Spanish speakers, she tried to follow what was being said and how much she understood of it. There were varying degrees of success with the latter but she mostly got the gist if it wasn't said at lightning speed.

On this occasion at her 'happy place' Lou had found herself creating a new routine. It consisted of her marching into the sea and, once adjusted to the heat, having a good swim (and wee) before heading back out. There would be no towel drying off. It wasn't necessary in this lovely heat. Instead, after manually wringing the excess moisture from her hair, Lou would grab her tiny beach bag (containing purse and phone) and head to the kiosk for a shandy. In the queue she would be literally drip-drying as the sun beat down on her back. Moisture would be happily rolling down her naked body as she stood waiting to be served and Lou liked the reaction of those standing around watching this. It was also a good conversation-starter, as were her multiple tattoos, built up over a period of some 22 years, not that she needed one usually!

It was time for a bocadillo and whilst the choice of filling and the quality was limited, it did fill a hole, so to speak, plus it was convenient. Munching away there she noticed Chris and Doris (the more mature couple she had met almost three years before [*in Vanilla Extract*]) and she made her way over to greet them. Lou did love reconnecting with people she knew and given they were the first people she had ever stood naked with at this very spot, they were met with hugs and kisses. It was good to see them again and their conversation continued seamlessly despite the time apart.

You were always guaranteed a good laugh with this cheeky pair and they were soon reminiscing about Pablo and other interesting encounters. They had some good stories of their own and were a font of information about other kiosk attendees: whether it was about their lives at their respective homes (whichever country that was) or about shenanigans that the couple had witnessed at the beach. It was hard to shock them, given all their experience, and Lou was finding herself in that camp too. With the various adventures and misadventures she had been a part of, she was less and less astounded these days; maybe amused more so.

Carlos was standing at the bar too. Was his name really Carlos? Was it Tommy? Who knew and who really cared?

So many people here had alter egos, pseudonyms, or just made up identities, but the reality was: it really didn't matter. He worked at one of the swinging clubs behind the bar and he had a naughty smile. Lisa was also there and Lou and her struck up an immediate connection. They shared a similar sense of humour and Carlos was surprised to find they had only just met there and then, given how much laughter was being generated. He also became the centre of that for a while as the three bounced off each other's wit. This was turning out to be a funny afternoon. Lou loved spontaneous times like this that were unplanned but just fell into perfect place.

After a group of seven fully dressed Marvel action heroes were served at the bar, some new visitors from the gay beach arrived for drinks. One of those stood out from the rest on account of his beautiful blue and white short bobbed wig. His eye makeup was over exaggerated and matched the colour of the hairpiece, with gloriously long eyelashes applied. The rest of the outfit consisted of a black sequin vest and a short blue patterned skirt. There was no mistaking this person was born male, particularly as his extensively large penis was dangling down at least three inches longer than his outfit! He was well aware of this too, as he shook it about for all to see. He was certainly a character and a good networker, as Lou watched him meander between the various groups at the bar.

Being a social butterfly herself, it wasn't long before these two collided in mutual praise. Lou complimented him (Fred) on his outfit, he did the same about her figure and so the discovery began. They were two very different people with equally dissimilar stories and here their paths had collided. She was fascinated to ask if it was a man or woman Fred was married to, when he revealed that part of his life and where they were now? He said it was actually his very much female wife (Mary) who had helped him put his eyelashes on earlier. Lou found this fascinating. She loved to hear about the different lives people led. Mary was only too happy to help in this way, but preferred to be relaxing back at the hotel rather than getting any more involved in her husband's mischief. She knew he played too, but he didn't quite share the extent of this with her. Lou wasn't sure if that was in relation to the variety of his conquests or the frequency, and she was certainly not there to judge. That was not her place not her inclination. Whatever made them both happy, and this certainly felt that way to her.

Lou couldn't help but draw attention to his rather ample manhood, which delighted him so much that he swung it around, past the skirt, and showed her the intricate strap and ring he was wearing beneath. "Well you're certainly blessed down there, aren't you?" Lou commented and Fred was overtly proud. Why wouldn't he be? It was immense! "If only I could use it more!" He retorted and so the jokes continued. He had a cracking sense of humour.

Lou wasn't quite sure how to react to his next comment about her own genitalia, once they'd established that he was bisexual. "I love your protrusions." It was a backhanded compliment that Lou didn't quite know how to take when she worked out what he was talking about. Lou initially wondered if he meant her pubic bone, but that didn't really stick out. In fact she had only been complimented a couple of days before about how neat

121

and tidy that area was, with no rolls of fat overhanging that you'd have to get past when giving oral. What she realised he was talking about on this occasion was her labia and according to Fred, if he'd been born female, he'd have wanted them like hers. 'How funny?' Lou thought. Isn't it interesting what different people notice and think? She went on to describe how years ago she had watched a documentary about women having those lips surgically reduced. (Amusing too that there's an industry now doing the opposite to the facial lips!) It was something she had considered very briefly but was glad she had left nature alone, particularly because some men like to suck on them whilst giving her oral pleasure. For a brief moment Lou became self-conscious about her form, but it soon passed. Subconsciously she had a quick chat with herself about how comfortable she was in her skin, even if some of it looked a little different after having four children. Suddenly Lou's world was instantly realigned. Lou reminded herself that it's just not worth worrying about these things - so she didn't!

The banter was so funny this afternoon. Everyone was on top form, so much so that they totally forgot about the parade and going back to watch it. Lou wasn't fussed as she'd experienced it a few times, plus she needed those final sun rays and vitamin D fix before finding herself back in England's green and pleasant lands. The beers (and in Lou's case, shandies) were flowing and despite the watered-down version, Lou was feeling a little tipsy.

They were soon losing the sunshine and Carlos gave very clear indications that it would soon return from behind the clouds if they trusted him. Many other sun worshippers had their own views on this and clearly hadn't heard his predictions, as they packed up and left the beach in search of warmer surroundings. Fortunately, Lou and Lisa's gamble paid off. Some 35 minutes later, lo and behold, the blazing sun returned to warm their naked bodies and Carlos was full of witty self-satisfaction. He was growing on Lou. The humour and cute face were certainly paying dividends and she wasn't blaming it on the booze.

After enjoying the very last of the sunshine, Lou decided to walk back to her apartment. Lisa and Carlos were leaving too, so they decided to embark on the dunes' trek together, continuing their banter as they departed the beach. In fact it didn't stop until they were outside Lou's apartment, which was first on route. Lou wasn't quite sure what would be occurring next. Given she had arranged to meet Carlos at the beach, did he expect to go to her place now or was he heading home too? Lisa was keen to get to her own place and pack as she was also leaving the following morning. Lou was in two minds. She could either invite Carlos upstairs to have some fun or she could let him continue walking to his own pad to relax before getting himself ready for work. Oh the dilemma - what to do? 'Ah fuck it,' she thought as she asked him if he wanted to come inside. It took no time at all for him to decide. It was an overwhelming yes from him and they soon bid farewell to their funny female friend.

Inside her apartment, Lou showed him firstly to the lounge area where he dropped his bag. The shower was the next stop off, where she suggested he go first as she made them drinks. Carlos seemed a little shy all of a sudden, but complied with her wishes. Wrapped up in a

123

towel, he soon returned to Lou, where a glass of wine was waiting for him. What a hostess she was!

Lou headed for the shower next. It was imperative to remove any sand from the glorious beach day they had shared. Lou was a stickler for cleanliness and protection. Despite her almost clinically clean record, there had been one incident where she had to take remedial action and it wasn't because she didn't use a condom. Unfortunately Lou was told she had contracted chlamydia from oral pleasure she had experienced a few months before. It was diagnosed as part of her regular sexual health check and Lou was faced with having to inform a number of partners of the bad news.

It was all very embarrassing and not one of Lou's proudest moments, but it was the right thing to do. This was certainly a wake-up call despite Lou knowing that this lifestyle would undoubtedly attract this type of risk. She managed to contact her recent partners and warned them of their potential exposure to it, knowing full well that one of them actually gave it to her initially! A course of medication and no booze or sex for a week took care of that, for her at least.

One of her partners (Roy) had recently had unprotected sex with his wife and was fearful that he had given her the disease. She had no idea about his extra-marital activities and whilst he couldn't be 100% sure, Lou was less than convinced. She actually thought Roy was the person she had contracted it from in the first place! Given Lou was a nice person, she was willing to help him resolve this somewhat tricky situation. Lou had her prescription from the health centre and she managed to order some more tablets for him online. It was up to

Roy now what he did with them. Whilst he could take his own medication, he needed to get some of those tablets into his wife's system without her knowledge. Lou was fascinated to hear how he came up with a cunning plan to disguise them as slimming tablets, knowing full well she would happily take them in those circumstances. This approach was going well until his mother-in-law also asked for some! It was a comedy of errors.

Another packet of pills ordered and this time Roy worked unassisted. Lou left him to it. He did report back that she had taken the remainder of the dose and he kept his fingers crossed that it had all worked. Having said that, there was no proof she had it at all, but Roy had to be sure.

So it was safe to say, that Lou did try to maintain her clean sexual health. Oral pleasure sadly was never 100% safe unless you did it through a condom, and where was the fun in that? The quarterly check-ups were hardly preventative, but they did give Lou peace of mind, in the short term any way.

Lou was not prepared to take any unnecessary risks and always insisted on using condoms (apart from for oral), unless it was a someone special in her life who had surpassed her 'privileged access' criteria. *(Vanilla Extract readers will know that meant someone who Lou had built up a more meaningful relationship with; someone she saw regularly and trusted implicitly.)*

Carlos had opened the balcony doors and was sitting out watching the sun rapidly burning the sky orange as it descended. When Lou returned from the shower, he was halfway through his wine, with the towel firmly tied around his waist. Lou collected her wine on the way and sat down next to him. It would have made for a romantic moment if she had been into him in that way, but if she was honest with herself, she knew she just wanted to use him for sex. As fickle as that sounded, Lou knew that's exactly what he was there for too. There was no pretense. It was fact. Both of them wanted to fuck and that's exactly what they were going to do.

His body was toned, but not the most muscly she'd experienced before. Despite it being a little awkward to start, Lou decided to take action and once the small talk and wine had finished, she began to kiss him. His lips were soft on hers and she was surprised by the passion she was feeling in return. Lou had thought once he'd gotten over this new shyness, that he would have been rampant and taken control, however, whilst still being obviously excited, he was very tender with his kissing and stroking of her skin. Maybe Lou had misread this situation? Perhaps he was into her more than she had initially thought and this wasn't just about corporal satisfaction?

"Let's move this to the bedroom," she insisted, as she got up from the sofa and moved along the corridor. The apartment was tiny, so it wasn't long before she was on the bed as he followed her in. Lou chose not to lay down, Instead she sat on the edge, with her towel opened. As he entered the room, she loosened his towel and it dropped to the floor. "Oopsie!" Lou churlishly blurted out. Carlos looked a little embarrassed but smiled at the cheeky expression he was met with. Lou pulled him towards her and placed her hands on his buttocks. Her head was just at the right height to give him something to help him relax, and as she nuzzled into his groin area he drew in a

126

sharp gasp. He was being very controlled given the circumstances, which ultimately gave Lou a challenge. She wanted him to be shouting out in glee by the time she had finished with him!

Carlos's penis was showing no signs of trepidation. That was for sure. In fact it was giving him away. There was no point having a poker face when that penis was poking out so evidently! Admittedly it had nowhere to hide and was soon in Lou's mouth, after some soft teasing around his cock before she went in for the kill! It was obvious now that he was a grower, not a show-er, which only added to Lou's fascination and desire to experience this impending conquest and for him to be exactly where she wanted him: inside her.

Carlos was enjoying the attention she was generously dishing out. He appeared a little surprised but ultra-contented at the same time. His pleasure he could not hide, as the pre-cum began to trickle out of the tip of his cock, soon lapped up by Lou and mixed in with her own saliva as she lubricated him, ready for her right hand to come up and cup his balls. Carlos sighed as she then grabbed his member with her left and gave it a firm grip. His eyes flashed open and he looked down at her in surprise. It was a sudden reaction in case Lou was going to hurt him, which of course she wasn't. Instead she rolled her clenched hand up and down his shaft. He relaxed into it and was soon moaning in content. Lou did this a number of times before she moved herself further back onto the bed.

Carlos instinctively joined her and made his way to her sunbaked body: straight to her inner thighs, which he grabbed with both hands and drew himself up to her awaiting pussy. There was no real teasing or playing, but straight in for the kill. He licked either side of her clit and then forcefully slipped his tongue straight up inside her. Lou hadn't anticipated this direct action and as a result she had to catch her own breath, which in turn fueled his excitement. Like the cat that got the cream, Carlos was on a mission not to waste a drop and there was certainly no objection from Lou. He could stay down there just as long as he liked, as she did love the attention, although he had other ideas. Not knowing him well enough to voice her opinions on his short oral performance, Lou went with the flow when he wanted to get on with business. This was all a bonus any way, considering she wasn't that fussed earlier at the thought of sex this evening before she went out.

Lou also knew why she wasn't particularly excited at this prospect, even though she was now immersed within it. Someone else was playing on her mind, whether she liked it or not. He was there and wasn't moving any, despite what she was getting up to. Was she testing herself? Was she wondering how she would feel after this event? Would it make her want this other man more or less? Or would it not make any difference? 'Shut up brain,' she told herself. She would deal with the aftermath after the sex – after all, that's exactly what it was.

For now, Lou would appreciate the moment. It was enjoyable after all and her body was responding in all the right ways. She would definitely come, probably with a little of her own manual intervention, which wasn't a problem. Carlos unquestionably would orgasm too; that was a given. It was more a case of when, as far as Lou was concerned, however terrible that sounded. She would appreciate it for what it was; a random fuck with a cute guy, with both of them fulfilling their carnal needs.

A number of positions were played out on the bed once he was securely protected with a handy condom from his bag. Lou climbed on top and showed him her riding skills, digging deep inside and amusing herself by the changing facial expressions she witnessed from above. She got the impression that Carlos hadn't quite experienced it like this before, which would be novel and possibly unbelievable given the access he had to single (and married) ladies in Gran Canaria. He was bound to be a super-player, although he came across as quite innocent, which Lou thought was obviously a show. He worked in a sex club for fuck sake! If, however, he was faking the surprise feelings of pleasure, then it was a good act. Lou carried on and introduced her right hand to the proceedings to enable her to come quicker. It didn't take long. She knew exactly how it worked and she'd had a lot of practice over the years!

After Lou came, she rolled off Carlos and on to her back. There was no need to prompt him. He was straight into action and pumping her repeatedly. She didn't think it would take long as he had to get ready for work soon and she doubted he'd want to be late. To his credit, he did give it his all and Lou felt like she'd had a good pummeling before he came. Frantically Lou felt down below and made sure the condom was still on his cock before she allowed him to withdraw. Thankfully it was and she hadn't managed to work it off of his penis while they fucked. It was intact and filled, as he removed and disposed of it to the side of the bed. 'How romantic,' she thought, knowing she would be clearing it up and cleaning herself up in the shower as soon as he'd gone.

Until then, they stayed on the bed, entwined but not intimately, and enjoyed the skin on skin contact. Carlos was very gentle with her, stroking her arm as they lay together. It was only at that point that Lou thought he was quite sweet really. From what he was saying, she realised there was more to him than she had initially thought. She may have done him a disservice and now she felt guilty: to Carlos for not being as engaged in the act as he deserved and to the other man rolling around her head who she had some fucked up responsibility towards, even if he was married! God, what a mess!

It was dark outside now and her thoughts turned to the evening's events and the need to get some food before she went to the clubs. She would need some nourishment and some stomach lining before the final rounds of gin and tonics here.

Carlos tidied himself up, retrieved his clothes and made his way to the door. They hugged and had a laugh about the day as he departed. They would no doubt cross paths again later, both with a little cheeky glint in their eyes and a need certainly satisfied, for now at least.

Chapter 11 - Planning and plotting

It was Lou's first party at this new (or rather new to her) venue in East Dulwich and it promised to be a fun-packed, glorious extravaganza - as they all claimed to be of late. This one was organised by a lady Lou didn't know, but plenty of her friends from 'the scene' did. Two guys separately had asked Lou if she was going and as she had no plans for this particular Saturday night, she thought 'Fuck it. Let's give it a go!' She had nothing to lose.

As Lou had started to see one particular man a little more frequently of late, he would be the perfect person to go along with, however, she doubted his girlfriend would feel the same way, nor his wife for that matter. The sparks between Lou and he had been more than electric since their first encounter at a certain chic swingers' club in London. They had seen each other a couple of times since and she definitely wanted to play with him again. He stimulated her mind as well as her body and she was enjoying this new adventure they were creating together. And for that reason she engineered for him to 'just so happen' to be attending the very same East Dulwich party too.

Their combined scheming resulted in him arranging tickets for two, but not for Lou to be his accompaniment. Instead whilst he would be attending with his usual party partner/girlfriend, Lou was determined that this event would go exactly to her plan and he would be 'balls deep' inside her before the night was out.

Now who should Lou take with her? It had been a while since she had seen Lars. They'd stayed in contact on and off over a period of around three years now, but hadn't actually seen each other since she took him to dinner last. She had previously felt incredibly guilty for the way she had lost touch since his diagnosis (*which Vanilla Extract readers will be familiar with*). He had told her he was probably safer to have sex with than many men nowadays at such parties, given his medication and use of condoms, but despite that, Lou had been overly cautious and they had not played since.

Quite out of the blue, Lars had messaged her two weeks before and they had struck up their familiar Whatsapp conversations. It was all very natural and easy for the pair of them to start chatting once more, as Lou found with the majority of people she had slept with. Maybe it was because Lou was so liberated or because she and a partner would usually tend to have a light-hearted approach to sex and not take themselves too seriously? Either way, it was always easy to pick up conversations where they had left off – however long the period in between had become.

Lou decided to ask Lars to the party, to which he readily accepted. As it had played out many moons before, they arranged for Lou to drive to his apartment close to where she grew up and leave her car there for the night. They would take public transport to the venue after a few drinks and some reminiscing at his pad.

Lou arrived at around 9pm. When he opened the door, she was reminded how beautiful he was: tall, athletic and with those sparkling eyes smiling down at her, she forgot just how handsome this German hunk of a man was. She remembered too what a lovely spirit Lars had about him. You know when you just 'know' someone is a good person? She wondered why had she left him alone for this long? He would have been a great friend to have during this time, if only she'd let him.

They shared a hug and the conversation flowed, as did the prosecco. There was a feeling of mutual appreciation and respect. Other than the hug, no other physical contact was made as the clock was ticking away. They decided to save that for the party and probably afterwards too. As they found themselves lost in reconnecting, time was speeding away and it was now too late to rely on London Transport to get them to the venue ahead of the last entrance at 11pm. Instead Lars ordered an Uber and they were soon on their way.

It transpired that they were the last guests to be ticked off the list by the two men on the door of the East Dulwich mansion. They then accompanied them both inside and a guided tour commenced. Lou was taken aback by the luxuriousness of the property. A brief glimpse into the sunken kitchen revealed an open-plan room full of very relaxed party people all in their glad rags and chatting very comfortably with each other, as they enjoyed the music and light-hearted conversations. The rest of the house included an indoor swimming pool, gym, games room, massage area, various playrooms and sculptured garden with a fire pit and ample seating. Lou was impressed. It was classy and it was beautiful. What a place!

As anticipated (and prearranged), Lou knew a few people already there. With regulars from clubs and other parties there was quite a network that Lou dipped in and out of, and a number of associates were here checking out the other talent in the room.

What absolutely delighted Lou was her own entry to the party! (She really couldn't have planned it any better if she tried.) It meant descending a few stairs into the kitchen, knowing full well that a number of guests' eyes were on her as she did, including her new male friend. He was on the other side of the room, but their eyes locked instantly as she scoured the room in search of him. A nod of appreciation was shared as she continued the general perusal.

Her friend Rebecca was also here chatting with a few of the usual suspects, who greeted Lou as she joined them and introduced Lars. Time for some more drinks now and for Lou to really let her hair down. 'Let's get this show on the road,' she thought to herself as the first gin and tonic effortlessly went down.

Lou met the female party organiser, who was much younger than she'd anticipated for some reason, and the two male house-owners, who were dressed in rather flamboyant jackets for the occasion. One jacket in particular captured Lou's eye with its Musketeer-like tailored waistline and draping skirt. The crushed blue velvet and ornate buttons gave it extra panache and Lou was desperate to see what it would look like on her.

"Your jacket is absolutely exquisite," she complimented. "Would you mind if I tried it on?" He gave her a look of over-emphasised surprise and in his French accent replied, "Only if you are naked." Now given it was early in the party proceedings, if not that early on a Saturday night, the de-robing hadn't quite begun yet, so the room was full of fully clad couples and single ladies. But that didn't pose an issue for this particular party person, who craved attention and loved to be at the centre of it.

Whilst still in her friend's company and with Rebecca knowing only too well what Lou was like, she could see how this would play out. Lou gave her a churlish look and asked if she would take her dress, to which Rebecca kindly agreed. Lou then commenced undressing, to even more interest from her peers - which of course she absolutely reveled in. First came off the body-con dress, which had held her in the all right places as well as looking glamorous. The matching two-piece bra and knickers set was appreciated for a short period before they also were handed over to her willing friend. A few comments of gratification followed, which naturally she lapped up as she turned to her French challenger, stood naked apart from her killer heels, with her arm extended, and waited for the coat. Now it proved difficult for him to contain his astonishment. He was so surprised that he happily took it off and gave it straight to her. Lou could feel every eye in the room now on her, including that of the very man she so desperately wanted to fuck. This show was for his benefit as much as it was for her ego.

With this glorious jacket now adorned, Lou paraded the coat in the huge kitchen and took up a number of poses to demonstrate the flares and fitting. Once happy with the show, she removed the apparel, handed it back and graciously thanked him. He placed it over his left arm and hugged Lou with his right, smiling bashfully all the while. He turned to his other guests and said, "I think I've just found my next wife!" There was laughter throughout

135

and it was a brilliant moment for Lou, which she absolutely adored. What a shame she didn't fancy him in the slightest. He was not her type at all and he absolutely stank of cigarettes.

Lou commenced with putting her clothes back on, which was unusual for her given there wasn't really much point. Why bother when she knew it would soon all be coming off again? But her instincts were telling her to do so, and over the last few years, Lou had started to trust her gut a lot more. It was usually the right thing to follow!

The man she had arranged to meet there came over shortly afterwards and they began to chat as a group with Lars, Rebecca and others. Lars was keen to play following the earlier demonstration and Lou was definitely in the mood as a result. She was on quite a high from the attention, so they went to find a room, leaving the others in the kitchen, and it wasn't long before they were reconnecting.

Lou immediately crawled on the bed where a couple was already fucking hard in the missionary position. A number of other couples and single ladies were standing around the edge of the bed watching and waiting to see what would happen next. Lou liked those moments at parties, where people were sizing each other up and choosing their time to either join in with new people or play with the person they had arrived with.

Given Lou and Lars were old 'friends' there was no real need to decide the way this would play out. It was already pre-ordained way before they arrived here in South London. Lou wasted no time and immediately unzipped Lars trousers. She gently removed his erect and rather pulsing penis. She'd forgotten how thick and long it was. It was soon in her mouth as he sighed and looked up at the ceiling. 'Just like old times!' Lou thought, even though they had only actually slept together on a handful of occasions before this.

Right now they were both suitably warmed up and ready for action. "Let me fuck you Lou. It's been way too long." There was no messing about and certainly no more foreplay. The unquestionable lust needed to be addressed there and then! He grabbed a condom from his trouser pocket, slung his clothes across the other side of the room and told her to get onto her hands and knees. Lou happily obliged, as the memories of a few summers ago were instantly in her mind and her vagina! And there he was, almost instantly. Lars was bull-like as he slammed into her. Given she was so wet in anticipation and because of the antics in the kitchen prior to this, he was able to slide in and out with no issue at all. 'Fuck yes, that feels good!' She thought. How had she forgotten what a strong and solid ride he was?

As Lars pumped Lou from behind, she focused her attention on a new entrant to the room. Despite his scrawny physique, she could see his pants were overflowing. 'My god - what beast is he packing in there?' Lou wondered. He was polite too and motioned to Lars whether it was ok for him to unleash whatever was inside, so Lou could give it some attention. "Nothing to do with me," Lars responded with a smile, and Lou was immediately on him, pulling pull down his pants - which was no mean feat given she was being forcefully pounded hard and rhythmically from behind. Fortunately all three of them saw the funny side of this as she avoided head-butting his stomach at the same time!

137

Lou's suspicions were correct. This young fella had a ginormous penis and she very much doubted she'd get it all in her mouth. Ever up for a challenge, she decided she would have a bloody good go though, which is exactly what she did! God she loved a spit roast, especially as she was so turned on already. With one athletic Adonis taking her from behind, while she sucked on a horse-like cock in front, Lou was soon gushing all over the bed and all over the pair of the men as they swapped positions. What a bloody brilliant idea it was to come to this party tonight!

Neither Lars nor Bruno came, but they both had a delicious ride and were ready to have some more after some hydration first. Lou went to the bathroom and freshened up before putting just her underwear back on again. Despite being very comfortable in her own skin, it was a lovely set, so why not show it off again?

Walking confidently down the stairs and into the kitchen, Lou made her way to the counter where Lars made more drinks for them both. It was cold and refreshing; just what she needed after that pummeling! Her 'new' man, the one with whom she had plotted to attend tonight, was on the other side of the island, speaking with his partner and two other couples. Their eyes met again and he knew exactly what she had been up to. Would this put him off her or would it excite him? Lou didn't really know him well enough to answer, but given they'd first met in a swingers' club, he should know by now what she was like. Lou was eager to know just what his reaction would be. Had she blown it with him by acting out her desires so blatantly? It was playing on her mind. What would come next (or who, for that matter)? Lou was in the mood to party and she hoped she hadn't upset him.

Fortunately the conversation continued and during that time Lou noticed how obvious it was that Lars wanted to pair up again, but not with Lou. He was ready for more now that he was rehydrated and he took a particular liking to the partner of Lou's secret lover. Her voluptuous bosoms and bright pink hair were arousing his interest and most definitely his cock! Lou watched the scene unfold before her and was amused to find that this curiosity was mutual. She saw the eye contact maintained, the smiles go up at both sides, prolonged laughter and a flick of the hair was enough to know this buxom woman wanted Lars just as much as he wanted her. How very fortunate indeed. This would make the delicious proceedings even easier to orchestrate, with no additional skullduggery or deception required on Lou's part!

Those around this rather engaged foursome soon retired into insignificance as the conversations flowed, along with the alcohol and flirtation. It wouldn't be long before they were all horizontal – about twenty minutes to be precise. And with much haste, they made their way to the room Lou and Lars had occupied earlier. This time it was empty as party guests had explored other parts of the house and into the garden too.

Lars was impatient, as before, and led the other lady straight to the bed. Lou did the same with her man and the swapped couples were now kneeling opposite each other and kissing furiously. From hereon it became a bit of a blur for Lou. She gave the occasional glance to her left to make sure Lars was ok, but ultimately she was now exactly where she had wanted and planned to be way before this evening. Lars was quite capable of being in control of his own adventure, so Lou left him to it.

Being locked in with her man was exciting and stimulating. The scheming that had led to this moment felt rewarding, if a little sneaky, but here they were enjoying every delectable tingle. They may have spent a little too long enjoying each other's mouth, as they realised their partners were already sharing oral pleasure ahead of them. Was it obvious they had been lovers before or would it be seen as them just savouring the new excitement of their tongues entwined? Who could say?

Time to move on for fear of being found out. He turned to stimulating her gush gland by hand and the rattling around in her vagina triggered the usual flood. He showed no mercy and was relentless in activating the fluid. It was everywhere: all over the bed, all over Lou and he seemed to thrive in splashing Lars and his new partner. They were all caught up in their own sexual scrumptiousness and both couples continued to strive for more mischief as condoms were adorned and sighs grew ever louder.

He was deep inside Lou now. That thick, girthy cock was filling her up as he pounded her hard. Wow – she really was getting it tonight! Time for a swap around, but not of partners: just positions. She didn't want to let him go. Lou asked him to lie down (next to the others) and slowly made her way on top of him. This way she would be in control, although she wondered for how long. She'd found he did like to take the lead, but now it was her turn. Allowing her pussy a little respite from the continuous beating, she positioned herself carefully as she straddled his huge penis and descended upon it. He was right at the top of her innards and had no further to go! Lou would build this momentum up gradually and his murmurs began to reflect her movements. 'This may take some will power,' Lou thought, as she desperately wanted to ride him frantically, but equally she didn't want to spoil herself and become too sore too early! She wanted to make the most of this stolen time together and so she took it slowly. Damn, he felt good inside her. This calculated circular grinding was touching all sorts of nerve endings up inside her and it was making her body quiver and gush.

Next to them on the bed, Lars was also in control and was fucking powerfully. The bed was rocking beneath them and 'Pinkie' was shrieking in delight. Lou thought it might actually be her instead that needed a hot bath after this session, as her pussy was bound to need some relief too! By the sounds of it, there was no limit to her orgasm abilities and Lars was most definitely reaching the spot!

Lou was done now with the more sensitive, focused grinding approach. Her thoughts turned to their circumstances and given they were allegedly strangers till this night, it was time to move things up a notch. Not only that, but the tickling of his cock way up high was sending tingles all over her and she wanted to come hard! Lou slammed her hands on his chest and grabbed his pecs as she rode deeper and deeper. There was no going back. She was determined to ride this cock until she burst. Faster and faster, wildly frantic, giving it all she had – and there it was. A current passed throughout her body as it seized up and the almighty orgasm exploded all over him. Her vagina clamped his penis tight as the spasm took hold. Neither of them was going anywhere until her body relented and freed her grip of him. He looked up in dismay and then smiled as Lou began laughing. "Fuck me!" Lou shouted with absolute abandon, only then realising there were now other couples in the room who had been watching their activities. She couldn't give a toss. This was her moment and she was enjoying it to the max!

It took a while for her shudders to cease. Lou's body was in shock and instead of waiting for them to subside, he flipped her over and whispered in her ear, "Now I am going to fuck you Lou." And there, before she could even recover, her excitement levels shot through the roof once more. Fuck she was turned on. "Holy shit! Here we go!" Lou belted out as he began. It was the ideal conclusion in her mind! What could top what had gone before? There was nothing that could. Now she needed a bloody good 'rogering' and that's exactly what he was giving her. Slamming that fat, solid cock inside her, moving her into different positions to get even further in and pounding her hard. She was putty in his hands and it was perfect!

It seemed that he could go all night at this rate. Lou wasn't even sure if he was going to come at all, but she knew she'd barely be able to walk tomorrow if this continued. "Are you going to come for me?" she asked. He looked bemused. "Do you want me to?" Lou suggested it was probably for the best and they both laughed in agreement.

Next to them the others had already finished and were moving away from the bed, gathering their clothes as they went. Lou had barely noticed as she had enough filling her attention (and her body) right now. Their grand finale could continue without any pressure, not that there really was any with them, but it just meant they could relax even more. This allowed him to focus on the end goal, which didn't take too much longer to arrive, particularly after the outstanding performance he had already given!

When he obliged with her request to come, he withdrew himself from her, removed the condom and began to wank himself ferociously. He insisted on facing Lou. He wanted her to be looking deep into his eyes when he finally gave in to her. (Lou later likened it to what she'd heard some murderers do when they take lives and watch the souls leave the bodies. This was a similar moment, but thankfully all pleasurable and no one got hurt - just a little sore.) As he allowed the euphoria to engulf him, Lou watched with fascination. He was out of control and riding on the pleasure the orgasm brought (as it landed all over his stomach, bed and a little on Lou). A glistening dribble of saliva escaped his mouth at the same time but he was blissfully unaware of the additional escape of fluid. Lou watched until the end. "Well that was fucking intense!" Lou told him as she held him tight. Some nods in agreement from those around the room, echoed her declaration! Reality was beginning to return.

Routing around the edge of the bed, they located their clothing once more and headed back into the kitchen, where they reflected on their exchanges. Lou was satisfied, if a little exhausted both physically and mentally. Her planning had paid off and she had a huge smile on her face, as many at the party attendees were now displaying. She was able now to reassemble her outfit and remarkably wasn't looking too disheveled considering!

It was time to leave and begin the next stage of her evening. They said their goodbyes, continuing the pretense of only having just met tonight, and another Uber took Lou and Lars back to his apartment. Despite

143

being exhausted, she had no doubt they would continue on until the early hours of Sunday morning, which is exactly what they did, finally falling asleep just before 7am. 'Now that's what you call a good night!' Lou thought to herself as she drifted off to a most contented and deep sleep.

Chapter 12 - Rio really?

'Well this should be interesting,' Lou thought to herself. 'Is he talking out of his arse or is he being serious here?" It was the kind of question she dreamt of being asked. It started like this: "Have you ever been to Rio?" Whilst Lou had been fortunate enough to have visited a number of countries in her forty or so years, Brazil was still on her 'to do' list. "I haven't been to anywhere in South America... yet," she followed up with rather rapidly. He revealed that he too had not been to Rio, but he had travelled to a number of the continent's countries and had some very good friends based in Brazil. "How do you fancy a weekend in Rio?" Lou was quite taken aback, firstly in delight but then secondly in shock at the realisation of a 12-hour flight for a two-night stay was a pretty crazy idea. However, given Lou did love her adventures, she was incredibly tempted and when he said it was his treat, it helped her come to a decision rather quickly.

Lou researched the flights and booked her own return to coincide with his. He would be out there the week before visiting his pals in Sao Paolo and they would both meet in the airport at Rio de Janeiro. He would arrive first and with her safety in mind, was prepared to wait three hours for her to land. Lou was pleased with the arrangements and his concern for her safety earned him some 'brownie points,' which she happily told him about before their trip.

It's a strange phenomenon to be getting excited when the person you're sharing the adventure with is already there - or at least a little closer to there than Lou was. Nevertheless, she still had trouble containing her delight. In fact the reality of what she was embarking upon only really hit her when she sat on the very last seat of the British Airways flight at noon on that Friday, when she accepted she wouldn't actually be landing until midnight (UK time). 'What am I doing? Am I completely bonkers? Twelve hours in the air both ways for a weekend away?' It was a crazy scenario, but a few gin and tonics later and Lou began to relax into it. It was time to accept that this remarkable and hopefully fantastic journey had just begun!

Lou soon made friends with the cabin crew. They were incredibly attentive and very surprised to hear the details of her short trip, although they had heard of crazier expeditions, as she could quite imagine. An ex-lover of Lou's had worked as a flight attendant and had shared all sorts of stories about what some of the 'trolley dollies' and 'wagon dragons' got up to in foreign lands when their partners at home were blissfully unaware. The 'car park lovers' would have their own tales to tell, but once they landed, any shenanigans were forgotten or at least never mentioned again as they proceeded back to their usual unsuspecting home lives.

To Lou's surprise, one of the crew knew of a couple of swingers' clubs that she had been to in the UK and mentioned the scene in Rio. There was plenty of action to be had and that's exactly what Lou knew she would be up to when she went out over the weekend. Their conversation entertained each other as they recalled funny stories to spend the time of this long flight out of London's Heathrow. It certainly made it pass quicker, with their cheeky tale exchange. A few films slipped in there and before she knew it, Lou was starting her descent. She hadn't managed to sleep a wink, but that was usual for her. She didn't like to miss out on anything. Even if a snooze had been welcomed, her body would not have allowed it, much to her frustration.

They had joked about him holding up a card with her name on, when she walked through arrivals, but that really wasn't necessary. As Lou departed the plane, she said her farewells to the staff and made her way through to the bustling airport exit. She was starting to get excited now, but tinged with a fear of him being delayed for some reason and not being able to tell her as her phone was on flight mode. 'He'd better bloody be there!' she told herself as she came out into the open. It was mobbed and frantic: people everywhere and all wanting a piece of her. Approaches for taxis were abundant and it took Lou a while to adjust following 12 hours in the air. It was 8pm here and it was heaving!

As she scoured the busy reception, out of the corner of her left eye, she spied him. He was looking as cool as a cucumber. His tanned face was looking radiant and his hair was swept back. 'Damn, he's gorgeous,' she thought. He was dashing across the crowd to get to the small exit where she would soon walk though. It was a little disorienting for her, but once their eyes were locked into each other, she knew exactly where she was going: straight into his arms. The hug was well worth the wait too and it lingered probably longer than it should have done, but that was just fine by Lou!

Any remaining fatigue was now gone as her second wind kicked in. The same needn't apply to him as his body clock was already in tune. He had gotten over his jet lag the week before, so he was bright as a button. A shower would help freshen her up and lose that horrid film she felt her body was covered in following any flight. She could never put her finger on what that was all about, but she always felt a bit grubby after a plane journey and was pleased to have that fresh water running all over her body to wash it away.

The cab took them to the hotel he had chosen. Naturally it was stunning, without being over the top. Placed bang in the middle of Copacabana Beach, the night views to either side were jaw dropping and they'd be even better in the daylight. To the right was Ipanema and she took great delight in planning their next day of visiting both beaches. Lou also had a list of places she wanted to cram in before they left, including Christ The Redeemer. No trip to Rio would be complete without seeing him!

Given she was feeling rather perkier than before, they decided to go out for a stroll and take in the local vibes. Across the road and just up from the beach were a number of cafes and bars. They decided to try the local brew, which she had never tasted before. It was a potent cocktail, the Caipirinha. He had been becoming rather familiar with them over the past few days, but it was her first and she had to admit, she liked the taste, even if it was super strong.

The question now was: would they go out clubbing tonight given the long day they had both had, particularly

Lou? It was Friday night after all and they were here to party. Well that didn't take too long to decide! Their minds were aligned and very much made up once the first cocktail went down! They dashed back to their room and started getting ready for a naughty night ahead. Fortunately they had researched potential clubs ahead of travelling and had two potentials lined up. Looking at the events for this evening, it was hard to call which to attend, but some reviews they could read in English swayed them to one in particular, and that's where they would be heading just as soon as that taxi arrived!

Lou was not entirely sure on the dress code for clubs in Rio. The gallery of pictures on club websites tended to focus more on the carnival attire and skimpy clothing but no real gauge on what to turn up in to this type of event. She played it safe with a figure-hugging mini dress with a one-piece basque underneath. It was a sure bet; understated but elegant and super sexy. Obviously the killer heels made the outfit and she was keen to see what other people had on. She would soon find out. He chose a pair of smart, dark jeans with a tailored shirt and over that he opted not to wear the patterned, fitted waistcoat he had brought. It was not necessary as he looked dapper enough already and would definitely have been too hot.

The club entrance was elegant: a narrow, plant-covered arch with fairy lights sparkling in between the leaves. Posters adorned the closed doorways and promised erotica inside. No further words were decipherable to Lou. Her knowledge of Brazilian Portuguese was pretty much non-existent, but there was no doubt this was the right place.

Outside a smartly dressed man welcomed them with

"Hello uncle, come this way." This was somewhat amusing to them both and equally friendly all the same. "Come inside and let me take care of you. Anything you want, you come to me," and shook both their hands as he guided them to the tills. The entrance fee covered use of the facilities and drinks. There was no mention of food, unlike many European clubs, which Lou wasn't fussed about. She rarely ate in any of the clubs she had attended any way, with always having in the back of her mind how her stomach would react. The last thing you wanted in a club was for your belly to expand! It was hardly attractive and could also be uncomfortable!

They paid and were shown to the bar. It was quite small and they could have been in any bar, anywhere in the world. They ordered up some drinks and surveyed the area, which was the normal procedure. Now was their chance to speak about how the night's proceedings could go and what the ground rules were between them. It was early days in their swinging as a couple modus operandi and for Lou he was the first man she'd been with that truly meant it. A number of previous partners had said they would 'full swap' with others, but when it had come down to it, they were less than enthusiastic. He, however, was still in a relationship of sorts, where he did just that and had been practicing this arrangement for many years. This meant he was really an old hand at this. He had way more experience than Lou, although he would never have admitted it. Lou thought this gave her carte blanche to do whatever the hell she liked and she fully intended to. It was game on in her eyes.

As with all cultures, there are similarities and there are differences. Lou learned very fast that in a Brazilian swingers' club, there is no foreplay. When walking around the venue and getting their bearings, at least two men had their hands straight up her skirt as she went past. Normally Lou would have been a little more selective, but she never stood a chance! This was made ever more tricky as there was the language barrier between them too. Very few people seemed to speak English, which she quite enjoyed, as it gave even more anonymity and dis-association.

For him, he was a little more suspicious of the make up of the evening. One couple was incredibly keen to swap lovers, but Lou's man was cautious. The same couldn't be said for Lou who was straight in there getting down to business once she had ensured a condom was firmly in place. He, however, had a suspicion that the female wasn't all she seemed. She was incredibly forthright and actually quite bossy. He thought she was being paid to be here, as she was very keen to ditch her partner for him and he didn't like that she was only here for the money and not for the fun. It shed a different light on the proceedings and he wasn't happy about it. When she remarked about his Rolex watch and how expensive it was, this made him feel uneasy to the point that the pairing proceeded no further. Lou was a little flummoxed as she thought it was a foregone conclusion they would full swap and was therefore a little sheepish when she disconnected from this local.

They made their exit back to the bar and he explained his feelings. It just hadn't felt right for him and Lou acknowledged that she should have checked it all out first before jumping straight in. The communications between them both needed to be clearer. He wasn't angry or annoyed, just a little shocked perhaps that she had gotten involved so quickly! 'Oopsie,' Lou thought! 'Note to self' duly recorded! She would be a little more reserved next time, well to start with anyway.

Back at the bar, another super strong drink went down and they laughed about what had just gone on. Always an adventure when these two went out to play and this was just the start. Dancing was next on the cards, as they made their way through another arch (indoor this time) and a larger than expected dance floor was hidden inside. The music was pumping and the attendees loved gyrating their beautiful bodies to the beat. He was in his element as the larger bottomed ladies had assets he adored and they were readily being shaken all around him. He gave it his all too and got down to the music.

Another gorgeous couple was dancing next to them and were soon rubbing themselves against them to the music. She was a Latina delight: absolutely stunning, slim, with voluptuous breasts and buttocks! He must have thought his dreams had come true. Her partner was mixed race, long hair and very muscly. 'That'll do very nicely!' Lou thought and it wasn't long before they were indicating they should all go upstairs to play. A quick exchanged look confirmed to Lou they were thinking along the same lines. It was game on.

When they reached a playroom upstairs, the swap took place, however the female of the couple was encouraging more play between her partner and Lou than she appeared to want for herself. After securing a condom in place for him, she was keen to watch him fuck Lou, which he did repeatedly, much to Lou's delight. She did provide Lou's man with a hearty blow job, but from the corner of her eye, Lou could tell the other two would not be getting as connected as she was. By the looks of it, they both seemed happy enough with that arrangement. No one looked disappointed, but instead both appeared very contented and enjoying themselves. They were having quite a laugh despite the language barrier. Lou thought it would be rude not to carry on with this bull that was so eagerly pumping her hard.

This went on for a while and to be honest, Lou grew a little bored of it. She was continuously looking over to see if her partner was ok. He appeared to be doing the same. Their eyes had met a number of times and the usual visual checks were made. Both were fine but on this final time of making sure, they both acknowledged in that exact moment that what they really wanted to be doing was to be deep inside each other instead. This was fun and all, but it was way more fulfilling when they were interlocked with each other! That feeling definitely surpassed all other short-term sex highs they had experience of late, even if they were quite exciting and fun.

With that knowing look exchanged, they pulled away and made their excuses - not that they were being understood anyway! The language differences were now more apparent than before, when their lust for others had been stronger and drove them upstairs. Now, however, it was obvious to them that it was time to leave. They wanted nothing more but to get clean and be as one. This involved a quick cab ride, a very long soak and chat in their incredibly large hotel bath, and then the real lovemaking began. 'Oh yes, this is more like it,' Lou thought as he slowly and very tenderly drove his fat, hard cock inside her and they made love until mid-morning before finally falling asleep.

This would certainly be a weekend to remember as fine food, fantastic company and a healthy dollop of naughtiness was all thrown in the mix before they travelled back to Heathrow together following this whirlwind trip.

Chapter 13 - The main feature

Lou was beginning to understand her attraction to this carefree, limit-pushing, rather dashing man. He was probably as bonkers as she and he continuously made her laugh with his unexpected and entertaining behaviour. Tonight was no different and he surprised her in the cinema, on a dreary Wednesday night in Bishops Stortford.

They had planned to go watch a film, but it was at one of those quiet periods ahead of a major international public holiday. The film producers were keeping their best new works until the start of the festive period. The lull meant there was little to choose from, although Lou did find one film that she felt would interest him. It was based on a true story about a toy creator and the cast was well known. Lou hadn't expected the cinema to be this quiet though, and for the second time in her life, she experienced having the whole place to herself (and he).

They chose the slightly bigger seats at the back and sat bang in the middle, to gain the optimal view. If they wanted to chat during the film, there would be no objections, and if they were noisy with their sweet wrappers, there was no one to complain.

Lou found the film a little slow. It wasn't quite her cup of tea, but it was not unpleasant. He seemed to be enjoying it more so, but this didn't stop him feeling somewhat amorous, which was probably more about being in an empty theatre with no one to tell him off. From their youths, the cinema tended to be the place teenagers would go to 'make out' as our American friends would say. For a more reserved UK audience, this meant kissing and fondling in the dark. The odd grope of a breast was the sort of thing that no doubt had gone on in his world. Lou had been way more behaved than she expected he had been at that tender age and had pursued her experimental lessons later. Needless to say, she had more than made up for it since.

He mentioned needing to pop to the toilet and Lou continued her viewing, solo now in this vacant auditorium. It felt like just a few moments later that he reappeared and was standing at the start of the aisle ahead of her. With the screen brightly lit behind him, she could make out his silhouette but was unable to see his facial features. He bent down and looked like he had deposited something on the floor. Lou could tell he was laughing from his body movements, but it took a moment for her eyes to adjust to the spectacle before her. What was he up to? He became more animated and was now dancing. At that point, as his body twisted around, she spied his penis shaking freely! He was stark bollock naked ahead of her and was jigging around in all his glory. 'What a nutter!' She thought as she pondered on his moment of lunacy. No wonder he was a keeper. It was incredibly difficult to grow tiresome of his antics!

Lou began to chuckle loudly. "What are you like?" She sensed he felt a bit silly now and he started to put his clothes back on. "Don't get dressed on my account," she reassured him. The dark blue jeans were back in place over the black Paul Smith pants he'd already climbed back into. The light blue striped shirt, complete with embossed initials at the wrists, was now on but left unbuttoned until he arrived back to her. "Could you see I was naked?" He was unsure if the full effect had been achieved. "Yes darling. I was just shocked as to why?" He laughed: "Well, why not?" It was a good point that she had no come back for.

He returned to his seat and before covering up that bare chest of his, he lent across and shoved his tongue deep into her mouth. Lou hadn't anticipated that either but welcomed it wholeheartedly. 'Sexy beast,' she thought. He certainly did know how to turn her on. It progressed to a 'full on back row of the cinema' snog and before she knew it, his hand was down her jeans and straight onto her clit. 'How rude,' she thought, as another on her 'to do list' was ticked off. It led to her first time being 'fingered' at the flicks and then some more. 'Ah fuck it!' Lou thought. It wasn't like anyone would catch them out or chastise them: well she hoped not anyway and fortunately she was right.

"Stand up," he instructed. Once up from her seat, he moved her in front with her back facing him and began to unbutton her trousers. He slipped them and her lacy knickers to her knees and forced her shoulders down ahead of her. She was now bent over the seat in front allowing him full access to her most intimate parts. With fingers from his right hand inside Lou, fingers from his left crept around her and began to massage her bean. The dual action was making Lou tingle from deep within and it was incredibly sensitive. The circular motions he began made her squeal with delight. She didn't worry about how loud it was, given they were alone. As her juices began to build, an orgasm soon flowed, way quicker than it would normally, and another tick off that list was crossed. Damn he was good! She really hadn't expected this tonight!

With her body lightly fluttering, he placed his sodden hands on her hips and moved her to the head of the aisle. This allowed him space to stand up and take her from behind, with enough mobility to do his 'thang.' Without a seat in front of her to lean on, Lou bent over and placed her hands on her thighs. This gave her the support to take the impending pounding without being hurtled forward a number of rows!

And so it began, but Lou soon became conscious of the cameras she spied in the ceiling. She had never noticed them before, but then again why would she have? Normally she would be focusing on the huge screen ahead of them and not what was above her head! Maybe they were now the main feature instead? Under the normal circumstances of a swingers' club night, Lou would have welcomed such a scenario, however, being at her local picture house, where friends of her children may well work or walk in at an time, Lou felt this type of behaviour probably wasn't best placed. She withdrew herself from his huge cock and motioned for them to return to their seats. "Oh-hhhhh," the two syllables he sighed were like that of a schoolboy being denied confectionary. "Spoil sport!" he laughingly added.

Lou wasn't quite finished with him, despite her attack of self-consciousness and sensibility. "Well you have been very good and therefore you deserve a treat. Now sit down, relax and enjoy the show." His unbuttoned trousers gave easy access to his now dampened member, which she withdrew from his recently replaced pants. He was still rock solid and as she knelt down before him, it slipped easily into her inviting mouth. His hands were soon either side of her head and he lightly guided her up and down. It wasn't necessary in the slightest. Lou knew exactly what she was doing, but it gave him some comfort as well as something to hold onto as she built up his growing crescendo. Somewhere deep inside of him, he wanted to force her down hard on him repeatedly, but he just couldn't bring himself to do it. She was already gagging slightly and he had no doubt her eyes would be watery by now. The muscles in her throat had contracted and were tightening on him. "Fuck, that's good Lou!"

As the clear and slippery spittle doused his cock, Lou's hand came around and began to wank him off into her mouth. He tasted of her pussy's sweetness, being diluted by her own reflexes as she continued to deep throat him. Performing such debauchery here was turning them both on and the risk was ever present in Lou's mind. This added to the thrill as she continued the fellatio until he was literally ready to burst.

There were a number of reasons why Lou was happy for him to fill her mouth with his thick, sticky spunk: a) they had a trusted relationship and she knew 'where he'd been' sexually, and b) it was way more practical to swallow his cum whilst sitting in the cinema with no tissues or napkins. And so that was exactly what she did after she had built him up to the point of no return and he let himself go freely in the warm and wet surrounds of her mouth. Lou kept her soft lips around him, as she nourished herself on his semen. It brought him comfort as he rode the wave of orgasm and ensured she did not spill a drop!

159

Once the practicalities were dealt with, Lou wiped her mouth in a completely over-engineered manner, trying to resemble a seductive porn star move. He smiled and said, "Oh you're a natural baby!" They both laughed as they composed themselves and returned their clothing to a normal state of affairs. "Now can I please watch the film, without any further interruptions?" Lou asked him, jokingly. "I've been trying to watch it all night!" This was of course a lie! 'Well that was certainly a trip to the flicks I won't likely forget in a hurry,' she thought, and it had nothing to do with the feature film they had gone to view.

Lou had a naughty sparkle in her eyes as she departed, which was undoubtedly due to the protein shot she'd just consumed, and most definitely more about the manner in which it had been unexpectedly served!

Chapter 14 - Ranting, bullshit and woodlice

WARNING: contains ranting, bullshit and woodlice!

Lou had heard some bollocks in her time. She really had. The episode in question came from one of her 'woodlice'. (This was a term of endearment Lou had named those men who crawl out from the woodwork periodically in the hopes of a consensual fuck.) Some 18 months had passed since she had heard from Jez and here he was popping onto her Whatsapp without a care in the world. Lou had deleted his number ages ago, yet the app still showed his name despite the unknown number.

Bold as brass came the message "Hello beautiful. How have you been?" Lou swiftly read it and then chose to ignore it. 'They make me laugh,' she thought to herself. 'Like your life is exactly where it was when you spoke over a year ago.' How could men expect her to be in the same place, with the same outlook on life, with no man of her own on the scene? She found it all quite arrogant and presumptuous actually and he was by no means the only one to do it. It seemed to be seasonal. As soon as there was a nip of Christmas parties in the air, the old hormones would kick in and suddenly every man she ever knew would pop up on her phone, expecting her to a) want to hear from them, b) give a shit about them and c) to pick up where they left off; if indeed there was anything to pick up!

Not only was it incredibly selfish but Lou found it quite sad. It was rare that she had missed them, and barely remembered many of them, and yet they would embark on another attempt to get inside her knickers. Was it just a case of "if at first you don't succeed, try, try again?" Or were their existences so very worthless that they had to revisit the fruitless challenges they had pursued previously, before events in their own lives took precedence once more?

What undoubtedly happened would be that wives or girlfriends (or both) had found out what their beloved partner had been up to and the flirtatious guilty party had been brought into line. Another possibility was that he had found love and therefore retreated from the temptations of the alternative lifestyle. Either way, to disappear from Lou's life and then to reappear without batting an eyelid, was just plain bad manners. It was rude and not of the naughty variety.

With Whatsapp revealing Lou had read his approach and without response, Jez fired another message across: "You forgotten me already Lou Lou?" She knew that her picture wouldn't be viewable, as she had deleted him from her contacts. She decided to follow this up with, "Oh I thought maybe you'd forgotten me over the past year and a half with no message?" What a dick head! "Did you find love or did you get found out?" she asked him. "I was in a relationship, but that's over now." 'Surprise, surprise,' Lou thought to herself, knowing full well why he was now back at her door, as such. What a bloody cheek.

"Let me take you out for a drink some time to make up for the silence." Bang and there it was. No scruples and no shame, as if Lou had been sitting there waiting for him to make contact! This was the same guy who swore blind that he was allergic to condoms. He said it would cause anaphylactic shock, which would not entirely facilitate a successful sexual encounter! And so the bullshit continued.

Lou confessed she was seeing someone - more to nip this conversation in the bud. However, this just fuelled the fire even further. "I'm sure you could do better Lou Lou." This wasn't confidence being displayed. It was his ego inflated to the highest degree. "Maybe after the holidays." Lou retorted, not wishing to entertain his self-gratification. She also knew full well that he wouldn't be contacting her again, well not for a few months at least, until the cycle came round once more - probably when Spring was upon them and he had a horny line to throw out once more to see who bit.

And while Lou was having a rant about 'the scene' another thing she really didn't understand was married men who think fucking someone with a condom but not ejaculating is acceptable. As if any wife will think that's any better than their husband being completely honest? Do they really feel their wife would say "Oh that's ok darling. As long as you didn't cum, that's fine by me." Lou knew of at least two men who shared this fucked up philosophy and another who did just about everything else sexually, but refused to penetrate her for the same reason.

Men, please - your partner will not tolerate this behaviour unless you have spoken about it in advance and you're both happy with this arrangement.

And don't be getting the arse if your partner does the same to you! What's good for the goose is good for the gander, and all that!

Another woodlice had been trying even longer with Lou and Lord knows why he hadn't given up the ghost? Lou had even said to him, "Look, it hasn't happened in all this time. It's not going to happen now." This was some four years since they had first chatted at a Torture Garden Halloween event. Why he still tried totally baffled her. Had he no sense of self-value? She didn't have the heart to delete him from her phone contacts, as they shared a few mature conversations over that time, but perhaps she should? Was it that she secretly liked when he commented on her changed profile picture? It was usually a subtle compliment like "natural beauty." It was harmless enough, or so she thought.

On the last occasion, however, he took it too far. Out of nowhere, after she thanked him for his comment, he continued by telling her he had been having some fun with a white girl (with him being of Indian origin). Not being particularly interested, Lou commented with "Great." Sadly and with even less self-value, then came a series of photos of them both having sex. Her face wasn't showing but her spunk-covered breasts were. Another showed his cock entering her and then another of him wanking. 'For fuck sake,' Lou thought. Why the fuck was he sending her these? Did the other woman know? Had she consented to him sharing these? Lou had never seen him naked and didn't particularly want to either. She thought she had made that clear. Why would she want this at all? What right did he have to send her them? What result was he hoping to achieve? Lou suspected it wasn't the one that manifested. She was infuriated and he was going to hear exactly how much.

It took very little time for him to understand Lou's reaction and funnily enough Lou hadn't heard from him since. She decided to block him after his last journey out from the woodwork. One less woodlice to deal with and that became Lou's new process for dealing with them. Short of changing her telephone number, the odd one will randomly raise its head, but Lou's new pest control method seems to be working.

Chapter 15 - Mile high

It had been on Lou's bucket list for some time and now, with a milestone birthday heading rapidly her way, it was time to tick it off the list: Vegas! She had previously arranged to go there with Millie, but other plans took priority and Lou found herself questioning whether she would make it there at all this year. Millie had headed to Costa Rica instead with her sister who was also celebrating a landmark birthday.

When Lou's new man casually suggested taking her there, she snapped up the offer and jumped all around the room, unable to contain her excitement. She threw her arms around him shouting "Thank you, thank you, thank you!" He then very generously offered a sum of money and instructed her to get on with planning. What a treat! This was the way to do it.

With so much to do there in so few days, she created an itinerary of potential events to accomplish in their five-night stay. On that list was a helicopter trip around the Grand Canyon, seeing an Elvis tribute, a gospel choir brunch, rifle range and of course a little horizontal pleasure too! He had already told Lou he'd found two events that might just fit the sexy bill and asked her to get on the case and investigate further, booking whichever Lou fancied. As you can imagine, Lou was thrilled to start planning this American adventure. They were going to have a ball!

The trip soon came around and what Lou hadn't quite embarked on was to tick something else off her list before they'd even arrived. The Mile High Club was an idea on her mind for years but her usual short haul trips had toilets that could barely fit a slim person in to do their business, let alone two getting up to no good. Admittedly they were making the most of the free alcohol being served on their flight, and that was on top of the bottle of champagne they had already consumed at the airport lounge. It was a bit of a blur how it transpired but given they were childfree and 'on their holidays,' it shouldn't have come as a surprise that they were now planning to start this break with a bang!

Lou was to head to the toilet first. It was the one in between first and business classes, with a curtain that hadn't yet been pulled across. The plan was for him to follow shortly afterwards, give a special knock and then join her in the loo for some depravity. As far as they could tell, no one else had this mission in mind. The flight did include some stag and hen parties, but all quite separate and seated towards the back of the plane. With alcohol and serious flirting afoot, this naughty pair were destined to make this naughty episode happen before they arrived in the desert.

A little giggly and trying to look inconspicuous, Lou made her way to the normally innocent, functional location. Fortunately she didn't have to crawl over anyone to get out of her seat, which would have made her more nervous. Once in the loo, she dropped her skinny jeans and used the facilities - well, why not? As she was drying herself, so the knock came. He said, "It's me," and she opened the door for him. He looked as mischievous as

Lou felt: all sniggers and smiles.

Squeezing in front of her, he turned and locked the door behind him. With Lou's clothes already where they needed to be, this mission was already prepared, but he wasn't quite. Lou sat back down on the toilet, undid his trousers and pulled them to the floor. There was her prize, albeit in a state of semi-readiness, and it didn't take her mouth long to perk him right up. A few sucks and his cock was fully hard and Lou tried her utmost not to gag too loudly in this confined space. She didn't want to make it any more obvious to other passengers what was going on in there.

Lou stood up, turned around and lent down on the loo. She was already wet and it took no effort whatsoever to slip his penis straight inside. It felt fantastic: maybe more so than normal given the risky situation they had placed themselves in. Before long, he was pumping her as best he could in this confined space, gripping her hips and then shoulders to steady himself. There really wasn't much room in here at all! As Lou looked back at him over her left shoulder, they both shared a churlish look. Were they really doing this? It was insane really, but a whole lot of fun.

As crazy as this was, they both knew this wasn't going to be a full-on session. It was literally to cross the act off her list more than anything. He withdrew from her, washed himself in the tiny sink and then made his way back to his seat. After letting him out and locking the door once more, Lou also freshened up and returned to hers. Once sat down, they laughed again and Lou couldn't quite believe they had actually had sex in the toilet. Finally that deed was done and it appeared they had gotten away with it too!

A few more drinks later and the insatiable pair decided to repeat the process. Well why the fuck not eh? They were bouncing off each other's energy and passion, not to mention being even more driven by gin and tonics. It was reckless really, but it was doing no harm and not offending anyone. They probably were less subtle this time as when they returned to their seats, Lou was approached by one of the cabin crew who didn't look too happy. "Can you please go to the toilet separately?" he asked her. "They are for single use only, not for two." Lou was quite taken aback and nodded in agreement. She didn't know quite what to say. "Tell him I needed help and you were assisting me with my colostomy bag," was the suggestion, but Lou refrained. She didn't think that would particularly help the situation and she was already embarrassed, which of course led to more giggling like a schoolgirl!

Deciding to play it a bit cooler, they separately tuned into the same film, timing the start perfectly, they focused their attention to their viewing. However, the stirrings still remained and they weren't quite done yet. They found themselves back in the loo and having a third round of carnal knowledge. This time Lou exited first and as she walked back to her seat, a row of gentlemen began to applaud. 'Oh that's funny!' Lou thought and her immediate reaction was to take a bow, which she did confidently. There was no point trying to deny it. They knew exactly what had been going on in there. Well it was hardly difficult to work it out!

When he joined her, he told her how the same row of guys had just clapped as he came out of the toilet too.

169

This was hilarious, well it would have been, had everyone else shared their thinking. A different member of staff than before came up to speak with Lou. "Look, we think it's great that you are all over each other and everything, but we really would want you to enjoy your holiday in Vegas. You're going to have to behave yourselves until you get there now. Is that ok?" It was their final warning and rightly so really. Lou confirmed they would and he walked away. She turned to him. "Why am I the only one getting told off here?" She smiled and acknowledged it was time to act like responsible adults again.

They tried to watch the rest of the film, but neither could really concentrate. They decided sleep was probably the wisest way forward for the rest of the flight. Fortunately the alcohol helped with the that too and when they landed in Vegas, they chose not to impishly leave the plane, which would probably be the way most would do so, given their outrageous behaviour. Instead they walked with pride. In Lou's eyes it was an achievement after all, although it was probably more of a miracle that they hadn't been kicked off the flight or arrested!

Chapter 16 - Naughty recollections

Lou was feeling reflective and looking back at a number of frivolous years, she wondered what was next for her? Could this life of fulfilling her lustful desires be sustainable? Whilst she had amazing adventures along the way, what else would be a first? What else was left?

Sitting with her feet up on her coffee table in her lounge, the house was empty. It was her ex's turn to have the children this week and she was taking the time to ponder. It had taken her just over two years to feel comfortable in her company in her own house. In the past, if she was home alone, she'd think this was a wasted opportunity and that she should be out there having fun; which invariably meant out there getting fucked or fucking someone else. But now she saw these quiet times as moments she could relax in her own space, concentrate on her well-being and enjoy the calm. Maybe she had grown up, but more likely she was now more content with herself and had nothing to prove.

Lou was reminiscing and having a laugh at some of her cheekier moments along this sexual journey of hers. She remembered the time with Snake Hips when they were on their way back from the office. He'd offered to take her home in his BMW M3 and during the trip they'd become so excited that before they arrived there, they decided they had to find somewhere to stop as a matter of urgency! The desire was so strong that when they spotted the opening to a farmer's field, they jumped out of the car, leaving the doors wide open and got straight down to it! After some immediate doggy style, Lou lay on the ground and he pummeled her from above. It was frantic and passion-driven and the pair of them couldn't stop laughing, until he shot his load straight past her left shoulder and onto the ground. It was hilarious until they discovered they were scratched to pieces by whatever the green shoots below them were. They only spotted the marks when they got back to Lou's and showered off! It had been worth it – just to fulfill that urgent need.

Another time when nothing else would suffice was when Lou had met Robert for lunch. It seemed innocent enough: two friends catching up in a Canary Wharf restaurant. It was a public place filled with 'suits' as Lou liked to refer to them as. (These were the office types, some of which took pride in their appearance, but many wore ill-fitting apparel, which Lou found a disappointment.)

Pizzas were on the agenda and as usual Lou was ravenous. Where did she put it all? She did love her food and was never one for being fussy or picky and she was also notorious for her 'hangry' (*hungry/angry combo for those unfamiliar*) moments, where she wouldn't quite function unless she was nourished! Accompanied by a sparkling water and a Coke for him, they happily conversed for the entire time, even though they had seen each other the previous day.

As they both had a particularly high sex drive and it never took long for them to return to this subject, they toyed with the idea of having sex there and then. Obviously this would not be at the table in a busy lunchtime Canary Wharf restaurant, but it could be just outside.

"I'll go and check the coast is clear," he said and got up after paying the bill. "I'll message you." Immediately the adrenalin started to build inside her. Was this really going to happen? She was excited and nervous all at the same time. As she saw him walk towards the toilets, she looked around to see if anyone else was watching them, then laughed to herself – why would they be?

Lou gave Robert a few minutes and then gathered her jacket and bag up from the table. Slowly she walked towards the door. No message yet, but she couldn't wait any longer. She was too charged to sit there still. She checked her phone again – nothing. Ok, so she would head to the ladies toilets and hide in there until she heard. As she pushed the door open, the message came through: 'All clear – get your arse in here now!'

'Boom, boom, boom' her heart pounded in her chest and she could hear it beating as the blood rushed around her body. Lou turned around and headed for the gents instead. A middle-aged blond man came out and crossed paths with her as she walked along the corridor. Giggling to herself, she went inside. "Lou," he whispered, "over here in the cubicle." She hurried across and he opened the door. "Quick!" Lou needed no further instruction. She was inside and partly relieved, but the laughter was proving harder to subside. She felt like a naughty schoolgirl and here she was in the boys' toilets about to be very mischievous!

The act itself wasn't the best sex she'd ever had. In fact, it was far from it, but the thrill of being in there and up to no good certainly made up for it. In the end they had to abandon the doggy style, as they both couldn't stop laughing. Whilst he maintained his erection, there was no way he was going to come, so they took it for face value and enjoyed a few more minutes of pumping until they called it a day. They reassembled their clothing, checked the coast was clear and both exited the toilets together. Given their air of confidence and hilarity, neither cared if they were spotted upon their departure!

Moments with Ross were equally desire-driven too. When Lou was in a role where she had some spare time and a non-micro-managing boss, Ross and her would often take some naughty time out. Fortunately London has an abundance of hotels, some you book overnight and others you book by the day. The latter often meant you'd end up in a disabled room on the ground floor and you'd have a super huge walk-in shower, which was very handy to say the least. (Lou wondered if her friend Daz had similar experiences in these rooms? His wheelchair would fit with no problem at all, but she suspected he'd used the facilities somewhat differently than Lou was at that time. On second thoughts, she wouldn't put it past him!)

A fabricated meeting in either or both of their diaries meant Lou could slope off and meet Ross. As Lou was single, she would pay and he would reimburse her, so there was no record to be held against him if need be. The cheekiest of those encounters would be in the middle of the day, when a full-on fuck-fest would take place. Both would give it their utmost – well, why wouldn't you? They'd be dripping in sweat, demolish a bed with squirting and other bodily fluids, use up a number of condoms, then shower off and return to work as if nothing had happened. Lou would return to her desk, feeling satisfied, and with her blatant wet hair, should anyone ask, she'd blame it on a gym visit she'd never made. It was all too easy really!

Whilst reminiscing, Lou thought about that New Year's Eve party where she'd ventured into London by train. It was freezing and she made sure she was totally prepared for the cold. There was no way she could wear the full length, glittery one shoulder dress on the train and Tube as she would have been shivering from head to toe. Those heels she planned on wearing were way too high to put them, and her feet, through that ordeal. Instead, Lou finished her makeup, rolled up the beautiful dress and packed it into her overnight bag along with the shoes. Her delightful two-piece underwear set was already on underneath her jeans and jumper and with her comfy boots now in place, she was ready to roll.

Close to the luxury Fitzrovia mansion where the party was taking place, Lou met Rebecca for a pizza and a cheeky glass of wine. It was walking distance from the event and perfect for them both to slip into their glad rags. The transformation was completed. You would never have known Cinderella had originally turned up in her civvies!

What made Lou think about that evening now, was the blatant confidence she exuded in that situation. Her overnight bag was packed yet she had no idea where on earth she would end up sleeping. What she did know was that there was a very strong likelihood she would find herself waking in someone else's bed. That was the usual outcome if she chose for it to be.

Attending a swinging party at the turn of the year was bound to help her overnight sleeping dilemma, but what Lou wasn't prepared to do, was find just any old person's bed to rest her head! She still had her quality standards to keep intact, even with a number of glasses of champagne. At the very worst case, she'd end up at Liverpool Street station waiting for the Stansted Express to begin running again, a couple of hours later at the most. And she'd be sat back in those jeans and boots, wrapped up toasty warm. As the evening's events continued, this wasn't going to be the way this adventure ended.

As far as she was concerned, Lou did actually leave with the best-looking gentlemen at the party. He was charming, funny and very easy on the eye. He was also a little bemused that she was packed and prepared to stay out, wherever she ended up. They laughed about it the next day when he escorted her back to the Tube for her homeward journey. She was wearing what she'd left her own house in the night before, so no one would suspect her walk of shame (or stride of pride, as she preferred to say).

Chapter 17 - So now what?

It really had been a rollercoaster of a sexual journey for Lou over the past few years. She'd gone from taking her pick of whatever variety she wanted and nourishing the particular need of the day or night. A few six-month relationships either side of that had given her moments of security and 'normality' if ever there was such a thing anymore. She had unintentionally broken a couple of hearts along the way, which she felt awful about and that was why she had returned to her carefree, single life. It was safer all round and no one got hurt.

Well that was what she was happily convincing herself of until HE came along and made her rethink. It did come at a point where she was becoming a little less chaotic and a lot calmer with her sexual encounters. As crazy as it sounded, the 'lifestyle' was becoming repetitive. She could read men like books and tell from their initial conversation just what outcome would befit them, and that was even down to their Facebook approach, not even via a swinging site one! The predictability was becoming quite frankly tiresome and Lou tended just to remain within a circle of naughty friends instead of searching out new ones. She had abandoned the hook-up website over a year-and-a-half before and she didn't miss it.

Was Lou now ready to be tamed? She never considered that she would ever want to be, given how selfish she had been over the past four years and the experiences she had enjoyed, but she just might be tempted. The irony in this was that in fact Lou wanted something a little more 'vanilla'. Perhaps she had come full circle. Obviously this could not be entirely bland and normal otherwise Lou would grow bored very quickly. She would have to have some sort of outlet for her incredibly high sex drive, which is why a swinging boyfriend of sorts would be ideal. If they could go to parties or clubs when the need arose and have excitement with new partners, then this would be the happy medium that could address all needs. This would be the best of both worlds – enough of a traditional arrangement, with the support of a loving relationship, but the added naughtiness thrown in that Lou required.

This particular man certainly had an effect on Lou. When they were together, they had a real blast and she hadn't laughed this much for years. He had taken her to swanky restaurants in London she had never heard of, and to countries she had only ever dreamt of visiting, but it wasn't all just about being treated in this way. The sex was outstanding and he never left her unfulfilled. It was thrilling, different, funny and delicious.

"What should I call you?" Lou knew he never used his real name and she was curious what to refer to him as. He smiled at her and left her hanging for a moment. "You can call me The Winner." Well she would just have to see about that. It was a bold statement and she wondered if he would live up to it. Enough men had come and gone, with all sorts of claims (usually about leaving their wives and promising Lou the world). He seemed different and they had an absolute ball together, whenever and wherever they met. This is what puzzled Lou. When he enjoyed himself with her so much, why would he deny himself having even more of this with her? Why was he cutting off his nose to spite his face? There must be more to this story that he wasn't telling her.

In his defence, he had said to her very early on in their relationship that he would never leave his wife and Lou had rolled her eyes. Yeah right: like she'd want him to herself full time any way. She'd only grow tiresome of one man in her life, like she always did. "No one gets bored of me," he had retorted and she quickly responded with "Don't flatter yourself. I wouldn't want you to leave her anyway." She was being honest with him (at that time) and wanted to manage his expectations. He'd even joked that 'as his girlfriend, she would have to move house so she could be closer to him' and that was after their very first date. Lou had obviously made an impression on him!

As it transpired, quite unexpectedly for them both, with the more time they spent together, it was inevitable that they did fall deeply in love, so much so that it scared him. Sometimes he would clam up about the subject, and then under the influence he would openly declare how he felt. Sadly it was a love that would tear them apart, as their closeness developed and much to her frustrations, he was true to his word. He wouldn't leave his wife or upset the family home, despite how he felt with Lou.

Lou was torn. She was at the point in her life when she no longer wanted to be someone's 'as and when'. Her good friend Mark had told her years before that her exploratory period following the split with her husband would be for around four years and he was absolutely right. Lou had got that out of her system now. She had grown up since embarking on her sexual journey and while she had enjoyed the most exhilarating of adventures, what she really desired now was for someone to love her (wholeheartedly). With him she thought she had the best of both worlds, as they went swinging together and fully swapped. This meant she had her outlet for wanting new partners whilst maintaining a 'normal' relationship in the real world. Unfortunately he wasn't prepared to change anything else for her, which was a huge let down for Lou.

Despite loving him dearly, she deserved more than being his ticket into sex clubs and parties, and his bit of fun as and when he needed. She truly believed he loved her too, but only one of them had the balls to make big changes. Lou had done exactly that in her life when she didn't feel it was going in the right direction. She had instigated the dissolving of her own marriage years ago and had known this would have an impact on her children. But she also knew that her kids would have wanted both their parents to be happy and living a full life, rather than live a lie. They were resilient and they were fantastic. They adapted to change just as they all had. So when he'd asked her what he should do with regard to his home situation, she told him he was asking the wrong person. It was his decision and one he would have to make for his own purposes. Lou could not be held responsible for it. She had made her own harsh decision years ago, which had not been easy.

Maybe one day he would realise exactly what he gave up when she walked away. Lou had her own love to find, ideally with the caveats she and he had so spectacularly shared. His pricking around was standing in her way of finding 'the one,' if that person wasn't in fact him, despite Lou wishing it was.

Lou deserved to live a full and happy life and ultimately she didn't want to end up on her own. Her quest to find fulfillment would continue until she achieved that goal.

Everyone loves a threesome so why not add the two previous installments to your collection?

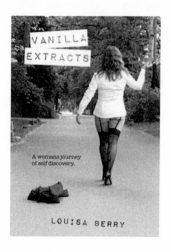

Collect the series from the bookshop at
www.3ppublishing.co.uk.

Louisa Berry lives in Hertfordshire, England with her four children. When not on 'Mum-duties', she works full-time in finance in the City of London.